I0597375

Also by J.M. Holmes:

Retrievers *(Anthology)*

They Left Me For Dead

The Fruit-Eating Cat

Energy Spike

A Deep Breath of Water

Waking Up Outside

Little Potato Fries *(collected poems)*

Pro Tem: The Amazing Year *(nonfiction)*

All titles also available in large print and giant print editions

J.M. HOLMES

ICE, ICE, BABY

LITERATI INTERNATIONAL
~ SINCE 1984 ~
Toronto • New York • London

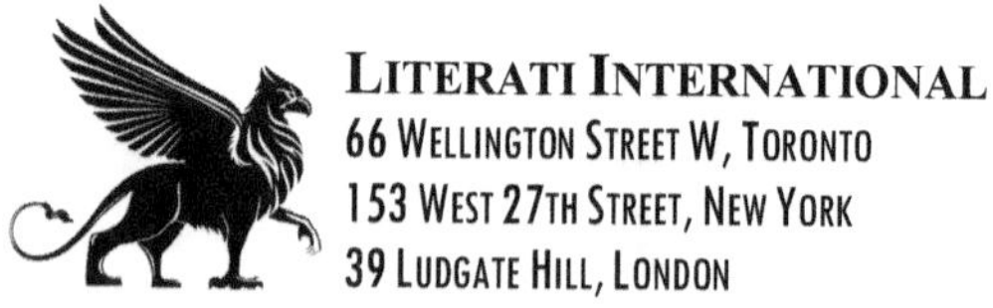

LITERATI INTERNATIONAL
66 WELLINGTON STREET W, TORONTO
153 WEST 27TH STREET, NEW YORK
39 LUDGATE HILL, LONDON

Library of Congress Control Number: 2021906237
ISBN 978-1-7368485-0-0

*To all those I left behind
in the Great White North*

TABLE OF CONTENTS

The explosion rocked the ship and threw Alice against the bulkhead as though she were a rag doll

ice, ice, baby

PROLOGUE

DOCTOR **T**IMOKHIN nudged his fingers together ever so slightly, and with a whisper the waldoes mimicked his movement, gripping the beaker in their mechanical claws. With a twist of his wrist, he upended the beaker and looked for the liquid to splash out into the isolation box.

Nothing. Not a drop.

Cursing in frustration under his breath, Dmitri Timokhin brought his hand down violently and watched as the beaker in the case shattered into thousands of pieces along with the frozen remains of the experiment.

With progress at this rate, they would all be dead within a week.

CHAPTER I

THE REASON the research party had been sent off to one of the remotest corners of the galaxy was fairly straightforward: tinkering with the building blocks of a planet's ecosystem was work best performed far, *far* away from any inhabited worlds.

The problem was, the scientists conducting the study wanted to survive the experience. But the way things were going, that was looking increasingly unlikely.

It had all started with Claude Boisset's work with compounds designed to super chill the ambient temperatures of their immediate surroundings. Besides the marquee application of restoring the Earth's lost icecaps at the southern and northern poles there were countless commercial usages involving everything from food preservation to building heating and cooling systems.

Immediately after his first significant breakthrough the corporate world sat up and really took notice for the first time; it wasn't long before he was flooded with proposals for lucrative commercial partnerships, and once the money started flowing the R&D really took off.

And so, under the guise of pursuing the altruistic goal of repairing Earth's environment, the Global Dynamics Corporation bought Dr. Boisset, his research, and his team of scientists – lock, stock and barrel.

The company converted one of their finest interstellar transports into a state of the art science facility and shipped the entire operation off to Tiamat IX, an uninspiring grey ball of a planet orbiting the star Rastaban in the Draco constellation, about 380 light years away from Earth. There the scientists could go hog wild with their experiments without any danger of contaminating an environment that humans cared about. And if events should go south, well, it was understood that the scientists were expendable assets. No risk, no reward, as far as Global Dynamics was concerned. And at least the scientists' families would be well taken care of if matters went tragically awry.

The first field tests were encouraging, showing a rapid spread of temperature declination wherever the compound was released. In the first 24-hour period ambient temperatures plunged by approximately 30 degrees Celsius in a five kilometer radius. The chilling compound itself was extremely fragile and broke down within 36 hours, ceasing to provide any further temperature modification.

A subsequent test confirmed the initial data, and the scientists began to compose their Nobel acceptance speeches.

CHAPTER II

"**K**NOCK KNOCK, anybody home?"

Vedana Narasu looked up from the technical journals spread out on her desk and brushed back an errant strand of inky black hair. She smiled at the visitor at her office door, but it was a distant smile, and her eyes betrayed her mind's preoccupation.

Vedana's scientific methods were old school, involving repeated redundant tests with meticulous examination of every variant in every result. Unlike her colleagues, she had been reluctant to celebrate at the preliminary findings of their experiments; for her, two encouraging tests meant merely that they were proceeding down a promising path, and not that they had achieved any measure of success. There were simply far too many variables left to assess.

Glancing back down at her desk, she peripherally noticed the knuckles on her left hand – the first two fingers showed red, slightly swollen knuckles which she recognised as telltale signs of stress concentration, as she had a tendency to absentmindedly worry away at her knuckles with her teeth when she was focusing on a problem. The redness of those two knuckles stood out prominently against the smooth caramel-coloured skin of her hand.

Vedana's appearance was striking, the result of the melding of genes from her pale-skinned Scottish mother and her Indian father. She thanked her mother for her large green eyes and chalked up her lustrous ebony hair to her father. The combination of the two gave her face a unique smouldering beauty to complement her svelte athletic body. That was a genetic gift as well, as both her parents were accomplished natural athletes.

Growing up at first on the Indian subcontinent and then later in London and Paris, she had always elicited admiring glances. It had been both a blessing and a curse. Vedana drew attention wherever she went whether she wanted it or not. Socially, that was a plus, of course, but in her professional life it was nothing less than a cross to bear daily. Her work had to be flawless to overcome the baser thoughts she inspired in her colleagues' minds – and that was equally true for both the men *and* the women she worked with.

Here on the research station it had become virtually impossible to maintain a detached professional demeanour. As spacious as the ship was, it remained a confined space where Vedana found herself in close daily contact with her coworkers. And while most of the women on board dressed casually, in leggings and simple tops, Vedana was well aware of the many "appreciative" glances she elicited when she wore similar body-hugging garb. She had added a lab coat to her daily wardrobe but got the impression that her fellow scientists thought she was just being pretentious, as if she were trying to advertise what a serious professional she was.

The worst of it was, a persistent malfunction in the ship's environmental control systems had been steadily raising the ambient temperature by several degrees every day. Repeated rebootings of the system hadn't helped and their choices had dwindled down to a complete shutdown of the life support controls – not really an option – to a serious discussion of actually opening a door to the outside and letting cooler air flood the ship.

In the meantime, the scientists and ship's crew had resorted to a gradual shedding of extraneous garments, until most personnel sported only a bare minimum of clothing more suitable for a gymnasium than a workplace. Even so, most were sweaty and damp a large part of the time and daily shower use had ballooned to the point where it was pushing the ship's water recycling capabilities to the limit.

In this regard Vedana was one of the lucky ones — a stint last year on Mackie's Mound, a desert planet in the Lacerta constellation, had necessitated her purchase of an expensive heat suit. It was, essentially, a skintight bodystocking that covered her from ankle to neck and wicked away moisture while using her body's own heat to activate cooling compounds woven into the fabric. Because it was designed for desert use it was pure white to enhance heat reflection, which made it blessedly easy to coordinate with just about any outfit.

As the shipwide environmental conditions steadily worsened, Vedana had worn it under her lab coat but was dismayed to discover that the lab coat would quickly become sodden with the moisture her heat suit was venting. She had resorted to wearing just the suit while sitting in her office and wrapping herself in her lab coat only when she needed to walk through the ship.

And now at her office door Manuel Delacruz, the team's virologist, stood smiling at her but his eyes kept flickering down to her legs stretched out casually beneath her glass desk, clothed only in the skintight material that left nothing to the imagination. She sadly reflected that even in her own office she couldn't be entirely relaxed, and she quickly tucked up her legs beneath her chair and brought her eyes into focus on the man's face.

Manuel had recently been showing interest in her that had nothing to do with their work and Vedana had been contemplating how she was going to handle him. She felt more than just a bit of attraction to him and probably would have enjoyed an extracurricular tryst, but she was conflicted these days. Although she was also drawn to another scientist on the team who had displayed signs of interest, her natural caution about workplace romances had muted her responses to both parties.

But it had been several months since Vedana's last relationship had ended and she felt sexual tension building up in her like a coiled spring being wound up tighter every day. She suspected that she would break down soon enough but waited for it to happen organically. They would probably all be here on this rock for quite a long time.

"Don't tell me I worked through lunch," Vedana said, glancing quickly off to the side to check the time.

"Well, yes, actually. You did. But it's not that," replied Manuel. He looked more directly at her face now and smiled warmly. "We want you in Conference 2 if you aren't involved with anything pressing. Claude has called a meeting and you weren't responding to the interoffice –"

Vedana looked over to her monitor – sure enough, there was a flashing red dot in the lower right corner.

"Oh damn, it was on silent mode, Manny. I'm so sorry. I was really focused on this paper."

"No biggie. It gave me an excuse to walk over here. I don't get out of my lab often enough. Gotta stay in shape, you know," he said as he patted his belly just above his belt.

"Well give me one moment to make a quick note" – she scribbled something quickly on a page in front of her – "and we can walk over together."

Five minutes later the two entered Conference Room 2 where their three fellow scientists were waiting. There was the team's other chemist, Dmitri Timokhin, their environmental engineer, Alice Prescott-Ames, and Claude Boisset, the team leader and inventor of the chemical compound they were here to investigate.

Dmitri was a small, wiry man who always seemed to be running on overdrive. He exuded energy and threw himself into every project with a fervour that suggested he was working to meet a fast-approaching deadline.

He was a perfect counterpart for Claude, whose laconic, methodical – almost plodding – approach to research would otherwise have been a stultifying burden that might have killed a project with its sheer inertia. But when he was paired with Dmitri the duo mitigated each other's behaviour to the point that real progress could be made on a short time scale without sacrificing attention to detail.

Alice watched them interact with a wry smile. She had been working with the two men for years and had learned to stay at a safe distance when they were brainstorming a project; eventually they would seek out her perspective, and her careful observations of their discussions were invaluable in shedding light on what they were missing or needed to change in their approach.

Her own expertise lay in an innate, almost instinctive prediction of the responses their work would provoke in the natural world. She intuited how living things would respond or adapt to specific changes in their environment on a level beyond mere scientific analysis, and adeptly surmised unforeseen results well in advance.

As a result, unlike most environmental engineers Alice was not trapped in an endless cycle of trying to alleviate unpleasant consequences; and because she was not constantly playing catch-up, her work was more productive with far more beneficial results.

Vedana's arrival in the room went unremarked as Dmitri and Claude continued discussing the problem at hand. Manuel had brought her up to date during their walk over: Lab 3 had been closed off because a controlled release of their freezing compound into a container of tomato plants had gone awry. It had been several days since the compound had been administered but it was not breaking down. In fact, it had continued to grow with such vigour that Claude had decided an hour ago to seal off the whole Lab module in an effort to contain the spread.

Dmitri was speaking rapidly. "It's not necessary to run another set of diagnostics – we've checked and rechecked every single element in that container and in the module itself. Every mineral, inorganic and organic matter, the air, the water, the temperature, *everything*. Nothing is different from the conditions outside on the planet, but the growth inside is increasing exponentially and shows no sign of slowing, let alone shutting down altogether."

"Dmitri," replied Claude, "Listen to what you're saying! Of course something is different. You can't have two different responses without changing a variable. We're just missing something, that's all. We need to take a new set of samples and examine everything again."

"That'll be hard now, Claude," interjected Vedana. "Now that Lab 3 is sealed off. There's a limit to how much we can diagnose using purely the remotes. We're better off examining the data we've already collected and searching for which variables might be acting differently despite the constancy of conditions."

The others all nodded silently as they considered the implications. The Labs had been mounted on the exterior of the hull after the ship had arrived planetside; all were modular and entirely self-contained. The inevitable conclusion that the scientists were now considering was the eventual abandonment of the Lab module by jettisoning it off onto the planet's surface.

"You're suggesting the Lab might be a write-off, Vedana," said Alice. "If we accept that, the entire project is in danger. If we admit we can't control or contain the compound, we'll never be allowed to release it on Earth. If we abandon the Lab that's the message we'll be sending."

Along with our own permanent exile, thought Vedana. She could see from the expressions on the others' faces that they were all contemplating the same.

"Let's not get ahead of ourselves here," said Claude, ever the calm voice of reason. "No one's talking about abandoning the Lab, or the project. We have a wrinkle, that's all, and we can think through it if we work on it.

"Dmitri, let's you and I run the data again, it's almost a given that we've missed something somewhere. Manuel, check your bugs right down to their DNA strands; it's always possible that they've injected an unknown mutation into the process that's causing this growth acceleration. Alice and Vedana, I want you scouring the literature for any occurrence of rapid unchecked growth in any aspect of any experiment that's ever been documented. Some overlooked factor is at play here – we'll find it if we search hard enough."

"I've had some thoughts on our environmental difficulties, too, Claude," said Alice. "And I'm wondering if maybe the ship's computer could be reacting to the sudden frigidity in Lab 3 and trying to compensate. That might explain why we can't tell it to stop raising the temperature. Maybe it can't separate the readings in Lab 3 from the rest of the ship, and it thinks we're all starting to freeze to death."

"An interesting thought, Alice. I'll pass it on right away to the techs who are trying to debug the system. I'd like to hope they would have already thought to check that, but sometimes the most obvious things are overlooked.

"The rest of you – get to work right away. If our two biggest problems are related, then that adds even greater urgency to solving the first one. I'm expecting 110% from everyone here. Don't let me down."

Wordlessly, the scientists turned away and left the room, each already deep in contemplation of the problem and the possible avenues of diagnosis. Alice caught up to Vedana in the hallway, though, and tugged her sleeve.

"Vedana, let's you and me go have a bite, OK? There's things we need to discuss."

CHAPTER III

**IGURD LOOKED** up from the surveillance monitor and stared at the wall in front of him, emotions swirling in his brain.

So far so good, he thought. Boisset's team was still completely clueless about the sabotage, and what he had just heard about their plans indicated they were nowhere near the right track for solving the mystery. A grim smile played briefly across his lips as he contemplated the imminent total failure of the project and all it represented.

He hadn't always been this confident. In fact, the results of his tampering with their experiment were far more successful than he had ever dared hoped. Before, he would have been content with merely disrupting their results and causing them a series of costly delays. With any luck that would have been enough to kill the project and return them to Earth.

But this unexpected reaction to his interference promised a catastrophic outcome that he had never expected. Of course, it also raised the likely possibility that the entire team – including himself – would be abandoned here on this godforsaken grey rock, consigned to spend eternity hurtling through empty space along with their environmental contagion.

The advent of interstellar travel had revealed an embarrassment of riches, as M-Class planets which had been previously thought to be few and far between were now found to be present in abundance throughout the galaxy. Consequently, the most unappealing and distant habitable planets with the fewest valuable resources to exploit were reduced to the level of garbage sites where mankind conducted dangerous experiments and abandoned the resultant toxic byproducts. Tiamat IX, their current unlucky locale, looked doomed to join the ranks of those planets unenviably marked as no-go zones. And if that meant his own exile as well, Sigurd thought, that was a small price to pay to save Mother Earth.

His fellow zealots back on Earth would agree with him, he reflected. Every one of them had pledged to defend the planet's integrity with their life, if need be. And now it looked like that was exactly what he would be doing.

For him and the rest of the believers, Gaia's dignity had been besmirched for far too long by meddling humans, and the adherents to the Faith were committed to preserving the planet's own native systems.

His heartbreak at watching his beloved Norway destroyed by the cascading effects of human-driven climate change had been the catalyst for his initiation into the Gaia Defense League. He'd joined the group when he was just 15 and in the ensuing decade and a half he had participated in over a dozen major operations against the European Industrial Complex. The individual cell he worked within was composed of only about two dozen members, and Sigurd had quickly distinguished himself with his ruthless zeal and passionate embrace of their cause.

His defining moment had been to take a leadership role in the bombing of a strip mine operation on Earth two years ago. His subsequent employment on a starship was standard operating procedure for their group – after any major operation the leading operatives went offworld for a few years outside Sol's system, the better to thwart any ensuing investigations.

He hadn't been back on Earth for more than a few weeks when the call had come for volunteers against this latest assault on the integrity of Earth's ecosystem. Sigurd submitted his name immediately. His skill set almost guaranteed that he'd be chosen:

since he had just come back from a stint as a junior programmer on another Global Dynamics starship, not only did he have an excellent chance at being hired by the ship but he'd also be in a perfect position to sabotage the project.

Truth be told, there wasn't a great deal of competition within Global Dynamics for positions on this assignment – there was a high possibility that it would become a one-way trip, as a failure to stabilize the freezing compound would mark them as highly toxic and render the whole project unreturnable to Earth. They would even be forbidden from leaving this planet for fear of cross contamination with an unsuspecting vessel enroute to Earth that might briefly dock with them.

For Sigurd, the consideration of their possible exile came second to the urgency of stopping this project at all costs. The goal of restoring the icecaps may be a noble one, but it was just another iteration of humans' arrogant meddling in Earth's environment, with each attempt causing even more disastrous side effects in the complex web of systems that make up the planet's ecosystem. The meddling needed to stop *now*.

Even if the Earth became uninhabitable for humans as plant and animal life dipped back into a multimillion-year cycle of extinctions within geologic ages of warming and cooling and eventual rebirth, then that is the path the planet must be allowed to follow. The galaxy offered more than enough other planets to ensure that humans could continue for millennia to exploit, degrade and use up every world they came across. But the Earth must be protected, and this compound the scientists were threatening to unleash on the planet needed to be rejected with maximum effort.

By the time the starship had arrived and landed on Tiamat IX Sigurd had already formulated a base plan for his disruption of the research. He needed access to the restricted science sections, though, so his first order of business had been to plant a Trojan horse in the security protocols that eventually completely crashed the entire program. As senior technician he was tasked with rebuilding the access codes and entry protocols, and he deftly wrote in backdoor access for himself.

His next step was to disrupt the experiment itself but he found this task more challenging that he had expected. The field tests were conducted on the planet's surface and the scientists jealously guarded strict control of every aspect of the project.

Two successful tests in row had left him thinking that this project had grown beyond his reach, but a lucky turn of events had put him back within striking distance. The scientists had decided to run more tests but this time in one of the lab modules. It gave Sigurd the proximity he needed to test a theory he'd been working on.

When his efforts succeeded he was overjoyed, but his respect for the scientific team tempered his optimism. Given enough time they would surely figure out what he had done, and he needed a distraction that would disrupt their work until it was too late.

He'd mulled all the possible roadblocks he might throw at them but it was a serendipitous chance system failure that had provided his "eureka" moment – one of the environmental control filters had failed in an Engineering section and he'd had to replace it and reboot the system before the air piped into that section became unbreathable. In a flash of inspiration he realised that if he could tweak the life support code to render their work environment uninhabitable, the scientists would be unable to investigate – or repair – their failing experiment.

But once he started digging deeper into the program, to his dismay he discovered that there was no separate code for just the science section. The ship had been jury-rigged to create a research vessel with distinct sections but originally it was one unified vessel and the life support program made little distinction between the various internal areas. His only option had been to tweak the temperature control protocols for the entire ship.

Unhappily, Sigurd had planted the malicious code knowing that he would soon be sweating his ass off along with the scientists. But the payoff had been worth it. Already he could tell that the science team's productivity was falling more and more each day as their work conditions slowly became intolerable. It wouldn't be more than two or three more days before the ship would need to be shut down and everyone would have to decamp to the planet's surface. By then, the labs would be unusable, the test areas would be overrun with the freezing compound as it slowly engulfed the whole ship, and the project would be written off as a total failure.

Sigurd sat back in his chair and began to mentally compose the progress report he would be sending to his unit on Earth.

The end is near, he thought, *for the project, for me, and for everyone else here. A small price to pay to save Mother Earth.*

CHAPTER IV

LICE AND Vedana sat close together, huddled on a small couch in a secluded corner of the commissary away from any possible eavesdroppers. They kept their voices low and tried their best not to look too conspiratorial. They were successful in this regard, as any casual observers would likely see just a pair of lovers in a simple romantic tête-à-tête, rather than a professional work-related discussion.

For her part, Alice wouldn't have minded injecting a bit of romance into their interaction; she had felt a strong attraction to Vedana from the moment the sensuous European had joined the team and she suspected that a significant portion of her attraction was reciprocated. Her tentative efforts to draw close to Vedana had not been rebuffed, and as the days passed she embraced every opportunity to enhance their physical closeness. Now, as they sat side by side beside a viewpane looking out onto the windswept barren plain outside, she rested her hand on Vedana's thigh under the table and was gratified to feel Vedana return the touch by resting her own hand on Alice's.

Nonetheless, Alice tried to keep her mind focused on the matter at hand as she whispered, "Vedana, I think there's something more going on here than simply an unexpected development in the compound's behaviour."

Vedana looked at Alice thoughtfully, trying to keep her mind on their discussion. It was hard, as almost the entirety of her brain was consumed with appreciating the warmth of Alice's hand gently fondling her leg, and desperately wanting to feel this sexy woman's hand move higher up her thigh.

Vedana's original efforts to maintain a professional demeanour in her workplace and to dress appropriately had been the first casualty of the inexorable climb in the ship's ambient temperatures. Although it was completely opaque, the fabric of Vedana's bodysuit was about as thick as a nylon stocking and left virtually nothing to the imagination. She counted it as a small blessing that all the other personnel had also had to resort to clothing choices so skimpy as to be almost salacious.

And it's not as though she particularly disliked the excuse to show off, for she admitted that she was at heart an exhibitionist. She took a devilish erotic delight in allowing herself to be so scandalously exposed, and it aroused her to sit there wrapped head to toe in this infinitesimally thin sheath bonded to her skin.

You couldn't wear any other garments beneath the heat suit without blocking its function, and the consequent sensation that she was essentially sitting here virtually naked, save for an open lab coat draped across her shoulders, thrilled her.

And since her suit provided virtually no appreciable separation between her flesh and Alice's hand, the woman's caress was now feeling so intimate it was almost electric, sending little tingles into Vedana's sensitive zone.

She had her own hand on Alice's and gently squeezed it, fractionally guiding it in the desired direction. As discreetly as she could, she slightly parted her legs just a bit to allow the other woman's hand easier access.

Vedana made no distinction between the sexes – they each had something delicious to offer, and she enjoyed indulging in both. But on a ship this small, with only a few dozen people at hand, she understood she needed to be extremely discriminating. It would be disastrous to move through a series of relationships with people she would continue to encounter several times every day.

But even though Vedana had kept mostly to herself and avoided any personal involvements, Alice had been pleasantly persistent and Vedana had come to excitedly anticipate their interactions as Alice gradually became more and more physical in their contact. At first, it was merely a briefly touch on her arm or her shoulder. But recently Alice had grown bolder, and now her hand was mere inches from the place where Vedana most wanted to feel it.

Normally Vedana paid little attention to other women's bodies and found her attraction to her own sex was more often based in the emotional bonds that developed between her and her girlfriends; but she had to admit she felt a strong physical attraction to Alice, whose gently curly copper-coloured hair and smattering of freckles scattered across her cherubic face was a comforting reminder of Vedana's clan of Scottish relatives. It didn't help that Alice exuded an raw earthy sexuality and had a tendency to look straight into a person's eyes while talking with them. The effect was both disarming and extremely erotic.

Like everyone else on the now-sweltering ship Alice wore the barest minimum of clothing, dressing in garments she had probably culled from her gym bag. Pressed up close to Vedana on the small couch in nothing more than short shorts and a skimpy tube top, she suddenly became a very desirable suitor.

She was a couple of inches shorter than Vedana, and a few pounds heavier, but that was mostly because she was much curvier. She lacked Vedana's athlete's body but was by no means fat. Vedana glanced down at the swell of Alice's breasts as they bulged above her tight tube top, and felt a strong stirring of desire.

Vedana brought her eyes back up to Alice's face and focused on the young woman's lips, pleasantly pink and glistening seductively, and just at that moment Alice's tongue briefly flashed into view as she ran it along her lips before withdrawing it back into her mouth. And while the only thought on Vedana's mind was how much she would like to lean forward and slide her own tongue into Alice's mouth, she found herself saying instead, "What do you mean? What 'something more'? What else could be involved here?"

With a conscious effort, Alice forced herself to stay on topic. "I mean that I suspect a human touch here, not a random mutation or a natural evolution in the process. I've noticed some small things that I had thought were just my imagination, but now I'm starting to connect the dots and I don't like the picture that's forming."

"Such as?" prompted Vedana.

"Well, for starters, there's the lockout failures that happened right after we landed."

Vedana remembered that when the system-wide access protocols had failed the ship's techs had had to rewrite the code and all the entry permissions. This was disturbing because there had been great emphasis before they left Earth on establishing a rigid security system to restrict entry to every area based on necessity and security clearance; by rewriting the code they had compromised that security, but they recognised they simply had no choice. Communication lag times with Earth preempted the possibility of getting the Global Dynamics security staff to supply them with new code, and by turning over that task to a ship's crewman the inviolability of the system had been lost.

"The following week I saw crewmen in the corridors leading to the lab modules. But each time I saw this I was unable to catch up with them to ask why they were there. I brought it up with the Captain – who, I fear, may be a complete idiot – and he dismissed my concerns with some mumbo jumbo about maintenance. I should have pressed the point, but at that time I had no real worries about the project – everything was going better than we'd hoped."

"And now you suspect sabotage?"

"I'm not sure I'd go that far, but I think we should be concerned. And vigilant. I discussed this with Claude, too, and he agrees that we need to keep our eyes and ears open."

"You said 'for starters'. Is there something else?"

"Yes, but I'm not sure about this one either. It's the security cameras."

Instinctively, Vedana glanced up at the ceiling. She scanned the room, but couldn't see any cameras from where she sat. Immediately, the penny dropped.

"Oh, so *that's* why you chose this particular spot for our conversation. I noticed you even tugged the table over a couple of feet. I sort of thought you were looking for privacy for… some other reason…."

Alice blushed. And then she smiled guiltily.

"Busted," said Alice shyly. "Yes, there was definitely more than one reason why I wanted to get you alone in a corner all to myself, well out of sight of prying eyes."

As soon as she said this, almost as a physical representation of her confession, she moved her hand the last few inches up Vedana's inner thigh and pressed her palm into the warmth. The thin skintight material of Vedana's bodysuit was less a barrier than an enhancement, and Alice could perfectly feel every fold and ripple in Vedana's flesh beneath her hand.

Now it was Vedana's turn to blush and smile guiltily. She moved her own hand up her leg and applied a gentle pressure to Alice's hand pressing quite deliciously into her.

"Good. That's what I was hoping," she whispered.

For a brief moment both women stopped talking and just sat there, breathing a little more heavily than before, both of them concentrating on Alice's hand.

It wasn't long, however, before Vedana suddenly clenched her jaw and with extreme mental effort forced herself to pull Alice's hand away from her. She raised Alice's hand up to her mouth and sucked gently on the middle finger for a brief instant, running her tongue along it. The she lowered both their hands and placed them on the table.

"That's enough of that, my dear. You'll have me squealing in public if I don't watch out, and then where will our professional reputations be?"

Whereupon both women slyly peeked around at the room and the various individuals inside it; but it was well after lunch and mostly it was empty, except for a couple of cooks down at one end, some ship's officers near them playing a game of poker, and one maintenance tech who had just now stopped in for a cup of coffee. No one was paying the least attention to them, and they barely elicited a prurient glance from the tech who had obviously noticed Alice's hand beneath the table and the expression on Vedana's face.

Alice laughed and patted Vedana's hand, and then suddenly became serious once again.

"I'm not sure if our reputations will suffer all that much – this is one of the few public areas on the whole ship out of sight of any camera."

"And is there another reason why that's important?" asked Vedana.

"Next time you're in your office, or for that matter, just about anywhere, but especially in the conference rooms or the labs, look for the security cameras. There are no lights to indicate when they're in use, but behind the smoked dome coverings they actively track movement and will follow you as you move about. That didn't happen before. They didn't start doing that until this week. I know because the servo motor makes an almost imperceptible sound when it runs, and my augmented hearing picks it up quite clearly."

Seeing Vedana's expression she quickly added, "My hearing was damaged when I worked on the terraforming project on Aldus Prime. I got too close to a tunnel borer just before it released a sonic blast into a mountain. The bionic implants that they gave me are about twenty times more efficient than my own ears were."

"But who do you think is monitoring us, and why?" asked Vedana.

"I'm still parsing that one out, and maybe if we work as a team we can make some progress. To be honest, I don't know who I trust here – I'd almost believe that even Dmitri and Manuel could be suspects. It could be professional jealousy or some misplaced competitive drive, but more likely money's involved. I can't guess whose, but it's no great intellectual leap to deduce that some other deep pocketed company would like to see this work go down in flames."

"Or freeze solid," added Vedana.

"Exactly."

"So what makes you trust me? Why can't I be the rat?"

Alice lowered her eyes a bit and grinned. "Maybe you are. I hope not, but at least it gives me an excuse to get close to you…. *Really* close."

Vedana cackled and tapped her fingers on the hand still resting in front of her on the tabletop.

CHAPTER V

CAPTAIN **J**OSIAH Latimer van Deep was proud of his family's lineage.

He was the latest of eleven generations of van Deeps to captain a vessel. The first of his kin to do so had been Captain Vincent van Deep who had distinguished himself with his courageous command of the *HMS Falmouth*, a 50-gun battleship that was responsible for sinking no fewer than *twenty-eight* of the enemy's ships during the War of the Spanish Succession in the early 1700's. Unfortunately, he was struck in the leg by a 3-lb. cannonball in one of the final conflicts of that war, and died of gangrene after suffering in agony for a very long eighteen days.

Captain Josiah van Deep hoped to avoid a similarly painful fate, and his current command of the Global Dynamics starship *Balboa* appeared to be leading him toward nothing more than a peaceful passing away in his own bed at a ripe old age.

And yet, notwithstanding his family's centuries of loyal service in Earth's mightiest navies, Captain van Deep was a rebel.

A chance encounter with a passionate member of the *Earth First!* eco-terrorism group had planted the seed in the Captain's brain, and for the last few years he had been slowly absorbing all the information he could find about the organization, and very gradually he had started to adopt most of its core principles.

He identified with the group's strong sense of outrage at the destruction that Earth's greedy politicians and corporations had wrought upon his beloved planet, and he decided that the time had finally come for the van Deeps to act in the service of *right,* not *might,* and he began looking for ways to offer aid and support to The Cause.

When Global Dynamics put out the call for a Captain to helm their science vessel on what might well be a one-way journey, no Captain in his right mind dared to throw his hat into the ring. But van Deep recognised this as his golden opportunity to redeem his line from their centuries of servitude to the forces of avarice and hegemony.

This so-called science mission, as the Captain saw it, was nothing more than yet another blatant move to exploit the Earth, and he scoffed at the idea that the company he worked for was interested in actually restoring any of the planet's natural environment.

If this putative "temperature modification catalyst" were ever actually allowed to be unleashed, he had no doubt that the ultimate implementation would involve nothing more than opening up even more of the planet's surface to exploitation. The only remaining wild spaces on Earth were in the defined "desert zones". Once this chemical was approved, even those places would soon be overrun with nasty humans, swarming the land like nothing more than a colony of ravenous ants.

Captain van Deep wasn't in contact with the *Earth First!* organization, but he was certain that they would have an operative on board, and the Captain determined he would do whatever he could to aid his unknown ally in their shared endeavour.

So when the security protocols failed in their first week planetside, Captain van Deep assumed it was a preliminary step in an insurgent action. He adopted a laissez-faire attitude and let the situation play itself out. He couldn't imagine what his anonymous confederate might have up his or her sleeve, but assumed that whoever had arranged the system failure must surely have a plan. The less he knew about it, the better.

When one of the scientists, a patronizing American woman who he thought addressed him as though he were an idiot child, came to him to report unknown personnel that she had spotted transiting through the restricted science areas, he dismissed her complaints immediately. He made up what he thought sounded like a likely explanation and was happy to see the back of her. Thankfully, she hadn't yet returned with more complaints – she must have gotten the message loud and clear.

But the current state of affairs was quickly devolving into ship-wide chaos. The environmental controls failure was threatening to render the vessel uninhabitable.

He was drenched in sweat underneath his normally-impeccable uniform. His Bridge crew were also drenched in sweat and starting to look quite frayed around the edges. And there was a definite odor of too many humans for one small room.

His Bridge was quickly devolving from its previous state of quiet command and control to that of a smelly locker room after a big game.

His Officer of the Watch, normally crisp and immaculate in a perfectly pressed uniform, slumped over a nav console in obvious misery.

The Captain preferred that his Officers wear their Summer Whites when they were on duty on the Bridge, but he was starting to rethink that requirement. Their uniforms were starting to look like they had all slept in them, and dark sweat stains mottled their shirts and pants.

Captain van Deep couldn't decide if the inability to reset the life support system was all part of some elaborate sabotage or merely the result of pure incompetence among his technical crew. He sadly acknowledged that they had really scraped the bottom of the barrel in assembling their crew complement. Very few people with any future ahead of them would readily sign up for such a mission as theirs.

But he was afraid to bring the hammer down on the technical crew for fear of disrupting any plan that might be in place to defeat the science team's mission. He knew that the experiment in Lab 3 had gone awry, and he crossed his fingers and waited for some admission of failure and the request to abort the experiment and to return home.

He watched a rivulet of perspiration trickle down the back of an Ensign's neck and he sighed. *Whatever plan is afoot, please let it finish soon!*

CHAPTER VI

AS SOON as she was back in her office Vedana couldn't help but glance surreptitiously up at the security camera above her desk. It was a pointless action, because the dark plastic dome that covered the actual camera unit masked it completely. She wished *she* had augmented hearing like Alice.

She pulled off her lab coat and threw it onto the visitor's chair in front of her desk; it had gotten unpleasantly damp during her time in the commissary. Of course, her body temperature had probably risen several degrees there due to the specific nature of their activities, and it didn't surprise her that the coat had absorbed enough perspiration to become soaked through.

Settling into her chair and shuffling through the research papers scattered across the desk, she thought about what had happened with Alice during their little confab. It had gotten way more intimate than she would have expected, almost as though a dam had broken and now their emotions were flooding out pell-mell. She hoped it wouldn't disrupt her work. This was a hell of a time to complicate matters!

Vedana noticed she was moving things around on her desk irrationally, opening and closing tech journals, stacking papers and then sorting them out again, and she realised she was overwhelmingly conscious of the camera above her head, wondering if everything she read and wrote was being recorded and examined.

This just won't do, she thought.

She left her office and walked down to Manuel's office in the next section over.

"Hey Manny, I was hoping I could borrow a cup of sugar."

Manuel Delacruz looked up at her with lizard eyes which bespoke his confusion at her remark.

"It's a joke, Manny. An archaic reference." She paused. "From about two centuries before you were born, on a world you never inhabited." Another pause. "I mean I need something from you."

Manny smiled and said, "OK then, that's something I understand. How can I help you?"

"You have plaster of paris around here for making moulds, don't you? I heard you mention it once. Although why a virologist needs handmade moulds I'll never understand – aren't test tubes and petri dishes more your speed?"

"The plaster of paris is for personal projects, Vedana. We all need some down time. Haven't you noticed my artworks?" He gestured at a series of small figurines on a shelf to his left.

"You made those? Oh Manny, they're wonderful! I had no idea! Still waters really do run deep."

Again, he looked at her blankly.

"Sorry Manny, I keep forgetting you grew up off-planet. I mean you've got hidden talents. I'm impressed."

"Thank you, Vedana, I appreciate the compliment. How much plaster do you need?"

Back in her office it was short work for Vedana to soak a few strips of paper in the mixture and, climbing up onto her desk, to deftly wind the strips of paper around the camera dome until it was completely covered.

Let's see how long it takes for someone to notice, she thought, *and let's see who comes to fix it.*

CHAPTER VII

AS LUCK would have it, it took no time at all for Sigurd to notice Vedana's handiwork. In fact, he was privileged to watch it in action, the monitor's image filling with her face seemingly staring directly at him in uncomfortable close-up as strip by strip she gradually obscured his view until the monitor displayed nothing but a blank screen.

After the meeting in Conference Room 2 had broken up, the only participants who didn't immediately return to their own offices were Vedana and that nosy American woman, Alice something-or-other.

Sigurd didn't like Alice. She was always underfoot, and twice had happened upon him as he was trying to get near one of the Labs. It was probably coincidence, but he was worried she might have picked up on something and now suspected him of some unspecified malfeasance.

When the two scientists had headed into the commissary the American woman had made a beeline for the one place in the whole room out of sight of his cameras. It was a double disaster, as the microphones were line-of-sight smart lasers that translated the vibrations in the air into sound; it was the only way to restrict the sound pickup to the camera's subject in a noisy room. Now he was both deaf and blind.

Frustrated, Sigurd had leapt out of his chair and hurried to the commissary, intent on seating himself near enough to the two women to enable him to eavesdrop on their plotting.

As soon as he arrived, though, he noticed that the women were quite definitely not discussing matters of palace intrigue, as one of them was busy fingering the other under the table, who responded by sucking on the first woman's finger. Clearly, their choice of table had been a matter of concealing their public display of affection from the cameras, if not from the human occupants of the room.

Simultaneously disgusted and relieved, Sigurd strode over to the drinks counter and poured himself a cup of coffee, and then left the commissary to return to his monitoring station.

The motion detection alerted him as soon as Vedana was back in her office, and immediately he discerned something different about the way she was acting. Nothing you could put your finger on, but it seemed as though her actions were somehow stilted. Sigurd had been watching Vedana for over a week, day after day, and had become accustomed to her natural movements. And her behaviour now was most definitely not natural.

She briefly left her office and when she returned everything became clear. Keeping her head down, she methodically prepared a paste solution, ripped some paper into strips, then climbed up onto her desk and proceeded to cover his camera.

This was not good.

He couldn't remove the covering or bring it to anyone's attention without betraying his surveillance activities, and of all the scientists it was Vedana who concerned him the most.

He had noticed her meticulous attention to detail and comprehensive fact checking. Boisset relied on her to cross all his t's and dot all his i's. She was his final arbiter who gave the stamp of approval to every experiment; if there were any flaws or mistaken assumptions, she would find them. Sigurd needed to keep an eye on her. That was no longer possible now.

He cursed silently at Alice. No doubt that little act in the commissary had been just that – a bit of theatre to cover up their plotting. He had been right to suspect them and he berated himself for having been deceived so easily. He switched his monitor feed to Alice's office to see what she was up to now only to be greeted by another perfectly blank screen.

Frantically, he pressed the rewind button on the feed and watched in horror as the display played back in reverse the last few recorded minutes, the view gradually widening bit by bit with the subtraction of strips of gluey paper from the camera dome, the screen slowly filling with Vedana's maliciously grinning face just inches away from the camera, until the image showed her climbing down from the desk and walking backwards out of the room.

He switched from feed to feed to feed, some were still up, another two had already been covered, and one was in the process right now of being plastered over. Within 15 minutes he had lost every one of his most important cameras and microphones in every scientist's office, in all the (remaining) working Labs, and in both Conference Rooms. Disaster!

CHAPTER VIII

MANUEL DELACRUZ leaned back in his chair and watched Vedana carefully wrap strips of paper around the camera dome above his desk. It was a little midafternoon entertainment that he hadn't been expecting. With the ambient temperature in the science station now up to 118 degrees, all pretense of modesty had been abandoned in favour of the most comfortable clothing each person could find. That Vedana's choice of garb was a skintight bodysuit that clung to her like a second skin was a development that pleased him without measure. And best of all, he reflected, she had finally shed that nasty lab coat that she usually hid beneath.

He sat there gazing upward, fantasizing about just reaching up and grasping one of the two perfect globes of her exceptionally perfect derriere so clearly outlined before him and so deliciously close. He had to tear himself away from the sight as he felt a familiar stirring in his gym shorts. He may have been consumed by lust but Manuel was no uncouth jerk and had no desire to embarrass the young woman with a crass display of his arousal.

Looking down from her perch Vedana had nothing to complain about. Manuel was clothed only in a flimsy undershirt and athletic shorts, and his skin glistened with slight perspiration. Notwithstanding his self-deprecating remarks about staying in shape, he was in excellent condition and Vedana snuck her own few surreptitious peeks at his nicely muscled forearms and chest.

She began to develop a bit more empathy for the men who usually annoyed her with their ogling. She reflected that she was perhaps twisting around and stretching a wee bit more than was absolutely necessary while she applied the papier-mâché to the camera dome and she silently chuckled to herself. *I guess maybe a bit of innocent teasing isn't so bad*, she thought, and did a last little twist around before she climbed down off his desk.

If she weren't already wading deeper into her relationship with Alice, Vedana would probably have been receptive to the obvious interest Manuel displayed. But she didn't want to be "that girl", and saw no appeal in juggling two relationships at once. Especially with coworkers. She was already breaking at least a dozen of her own rules with Alice and that was about as far as she was willing to go. Poor Manny was just too late to the party.

She glanced at the display on the wall by the door and momentarily twitched before she remembered that the ship's temperature readouts were in Fahrenheit.

"Good grief, why in the world aren't these displays in Celsius," she said. "I have to do math every time I check the temperature."

Manuel chuckled good naturedly. "It's an *American* ship, Vedana. Global Dynamics is an American company."

Vedana rolled her eyes in exasperation. The Americans still hadn't abandoned Imperial measurements for the vastly more efficient metric system. Even when plotting their trajectory in sub-light travel they still had to use feet, yards, and *miles*, for God's Sake! And because the entire scientific community used metric, there were countless examples of accidents and ruined experiments when the participants had mixed their measurements.

Even at the very beginning of the space age, Vedana had read recently in a technical journal, NASA crashed one of its first Mars Climate Orbiters because spacecraft engineers failed to convert from Imperial to metric measurements when exchanging vital data before the craft was launched.

You'd think they would have learned their lesson then, mused Vedana. But in the ensuing centuries nothing had changed and she gave up hope of it ever happening now. It extended even to the planets that the Americans settled, which were all firmly mired in the Imperial system. *Humans are such perverse creatures*, she thought.

Manuel stood up and peered at the newly-coated camera housing above his desk.

"Why, thank you, Vedana," he said as she brushed back her hair and self-consciously smoothed out some nonexistent wrinkles from her bodysuit. "I'm sure it will be very informative to learn why you've covered up my security camera, but I can't say I mind losing Big Brother's access to my workspace.

"In fact," he continued, choosing his words carefully, "Now that it's nicely private in here and shielded from prying eyes, maybe you'd like to take a few moments to relax so we can catch up…."

Vedana hated herself for pausing almost imperceptibly while she considered – if only for a nanosecond – the obvious overture. Her attraction to Manuel must be stronger than she had realised.

A momentary transient flash in her mind of stripping off his clothes and grinding herself against him sent a quick little thrill through her body, but her better self won out and she grimly smiled back at him as she said, "You know, Manny, I'd actually really love to do that, but I just can't… it's, you know, not a good time for me right now…."

Credit Manuel for being astute, she thought, as he quickly cut her off before the moment could become awkward. "Of course, Vedana. I forgot you told me you had more cameras to cover. Do you need me to come with you to lend a hand?"

"No, I'm good, like you said earlier, I can use some exercise too. It's good to get up from my desk."

Before either one of them could add much more Vedana quickly swept up her bowl of paste and trotted out of his office. Manuel sighed and leaned back in his chair, certain he would not be getting much accomplished now for at least the next hour or so – his thoughts were about as far away from his work as they could be. Maybe he should go for a run….

CHAPTER IX

ALICE'S OFFICE had actually been Vedana's first stop, and when she had suddenly appeared in the doorway with her little bowl of paste in hand Alice had felt a little leap in her chest as she mistakenly thought it was a social visit. *Come back for a bit more of that fun, have we?* she thought, before Vedana quickly explained the task at hand.

It was off-putting, Vedana wearing that bodysuit, thought Alice. Why, she might just as well have painted her skin white and stopped there, but in fact the suit made things even worse by smoothing out and enhancing every delicious curve.

And as she watched Vedana clamber up onto her desk and stretch up to the camera, Alice's reaction perfectly matched the response Vedana would elicit from Manuel a few minutes hence.

The only difference was, while the grammar of Manuel's thoughts was composed entirely in the conditional tense – the words "if" and "would" being predominant – her thoughts were distinctly grounded in the future perfect.

After Vedana had hurried out on her way to her next stop, declining all offers of help, Alice pushed her mind to concentrate on the mission at hand.

How irrational the human brain can be! she thought.

With everything that's at stake here, and it was all she could do to keep from chasing after her fellow scientist and ravaging her on the spot.

Well, fun was fun, but first there were life and death matters to deal with.

She turned back to her monitor and studied the data on the screen.

Alice was on the Spectrum. She presented well, though, so most people never clued-in that there was anything different about her. She had trained herself to look directly at people's eyes when she spoke, when her natural inclination was to look down or off to the side. Her sex drive was so elevated it was almost overwhelming, and she constantly had to work to restrain herself lest she sleep with every human in sight.

But her brain was uniquely wired to give her an almost supernatural skill at pattern recognition. It was probably why she was so intuitive in her analyses of complex systems and the variety of outcomes that external influences would generate.

She was most effective when presented with a vast array of data sets. She could scan them all in minutes and immediately discern patterns, tendencies, susceptibilities, and failures. Right now her monitor was flashing a series of data sets on the tomato plant experiment in Lab 3, and immediately following it with an identical series of reports on the two test runs they had conducted outside.

Like a savant who sees a pile of hundreds of toothpicks spilled on a floor and knows immediately exactly how many there are, her brain instantaneously tabulated every column and row in every report and picked out the variables that didn't quite match up. The problem was, there really weren't any. Every factor had been accounted for, and every condition considered. The experiments were almost clones of each other and there was no logical reason why the results should have differed.

But there it was, of course. The experiment in Lab 3 was exhibiting behaviour that neither of the other experiments had. The only explanation was unsettling to Alice and not something she wanted to accept: someone had found an imperceptible way to alter the freezing compound. Illicit human interference was the only possible explanation.

Despite the intolerable heat, Alice felt a shiver pass through her body. She reflected that they were all alone out here, almost 400 light years away from home, with person(s) unknown working in secret to defeat their project. Persons who would have to have a death wish, she thought, because they had to know that the kind of catastrophic failure they were engineering would doom them all to exile on this barren rock.

Such individuals were usually beyond reasoning with, and equally unlikely to confess. The team's only chance was to ferret out the malefactors without tipping their hand, and hopefully apprehend the guilty party before he or she could erase their tracks. If the scientists couldn't find out exactly how the compound had been tampered with, it would remain too dangerous to ever deploy on Earth.

A glimmer of a plan began to germinate in Alice's brain. *We need to set a trap,* she thought. *Something that will draw them out, force them to show their hand....*

She leaned back in her chair and closed her eyes in concentration. The solution was in front of her, she was sure; she just needed to see it.

CHAPTER X

 **P**sst! Vedana!"

The urgent whisper hissed through the air and made Vedana jump in her chair.

She had been lost in her work, head down, intently studying a technical journal on flow mechanics. One of her avenues of examination concerned the exact means of spread that the compound was exhibiting. Vedana knew that great insights often arose out of almost unrelated topics, and she hoped that exploring the physical properties of movement might provide the clue she was searching for.

The whisper caught her by surprise and she was embarrassed by how violently it startled her. She looked up and saw Alice standing at the threshold to her office, almost as though the woman were afraid to actually enter the room.

"Ali –" she began, but stopped as Alice raised a finger to her lips.

"Keep your voice down, Vedana," whispered Alice. "I don't know how many listening devices there are around here, but I'd like to take a shot at doing this quietly just in case."

Vedana said nothing, and just looked quizzically at Alice.

"Come to Claude's office in five minutes. Be discreet."

And she disappeared down the corridor.

Curiouser and curiouser, thought Vedana. *This job has suddenly taken a decidedly bizarre turn....* And instinctively she craned her head to look up the corridor in the other direction, almost expecting to see a white rabbit peering at her from around the corner.

I must be getting punch-drunk, she thought, and turned her attention back to her journals.

CHAPTER XI

CLAUDE AND **D**MITRI were already waiting in Claude's office by time Vedana arrived. Alice had her back turned to the entrance as she quickly jotted out a series of points on a whiteboard mounted on the wall.

Alice turned around as Vedana entered and asked, "No Manuel? I was hoping he'd be with you."

"I haven't seen him since I plastered over his monitor," she replied.

"Hmm, I wonder where he's got to. Oh well, can't be helped. We'll have to catch him up later."

Alice finished scribbling out her points and turned to the little group.

"First things first. We need to be aware we are being monitored everywhere we go. Maybe even in our quarters, for all I know.

"Take a look at that little device on Claude's desk —" and all eyes immediately turned to a tiny flat box sitting on the edge of the desk, with two green lights flashing beside a small readout pane.

"That's a device that came with my hearing implants. I use it to calibrate the implants every few months or so.

"It scans the immediate area and automatically links with my implants. As an unintended side benefit, it will also pick up any other microphones within range, which means it can function as a simple bug detector. The two green lights you see flashing represent my two implants. There are no other listening devices present in this room. We can speak privately here."

"At least since Vedana covered over my security camera," added Claude.

"Right. Most certainly the audio was part of the camera function and it appears she's disabled it completely. Probably some kind of line of sight pickup."

"Why didn't you just spray paint over the lens housing," Dmitri, ever the scientist, asked Vedana. "It seems that would have been more efficient than plaster."

"But much harder to remove," she replied. "All I need now to remove the covering from any camera is a bowl of hot water and some baking soda from the commissary."

"OK. So let's get to why we're all here," said Alice, and she turned back to her whiteboard.

"Let's summarize our situation: One, our experiments have been tampered with –" She held up her hand to preempt any interruption as both Claude and Dmitri opened their mouths to object, then continued. "I'll explain why I believe that a bit later. Just let's go with it for now.

"Two, the unknown person, or persons, involved – let's just call them 'the enemy' for short – the enemy is probably behind a lot of the things that have gone wrong so far: the lockout failures, the environmental control malfunction, and most definitely the experiment in Lab 3.

"And just so you know," here she paused meaningfully, "I've eliminated the possibility that the enemy could be any one of us – none of us had access to the ship's systems and we wouldn't have needed to defeat the security lockouts, either. So I think we can trust each other. But absolutely no one else on this ship."

She paused to take a breath and Claude murmured, "You've made a lot of assumptions, Alice. I assume you've collected some evidence to shore up your suspicions."

"Don't worry, Claude, I think you'll agree with my conclusions when I'm done."

"And I have to say, Alice," interjected Dmitri in mock outrage, "That I feel personally *very wounded* that you could have even considered that any one of us could be complicit in this sabotage. I would have hoped that we've shared enough over the years that you could trust us even without evidence."

"I'm a scientist, Dmitri. I take nothing for granted and believe only the facts I can verify. And *I* would have hoped that *you* of all people would understand that," she added dryly.

"Yeah yeah," interrupted Vedana. "Back to the meat and potatoes, Alice. I don't have all day here."

Ignoring the laughter, Alice picked up where she had left off.

"OK. Three. We've got a real problem now with Lab 3. We can't jettison it onto the planet because we risk releasing whatever is inside it. That could prevent any further experimentation on the planet's surface. Permanently.

"Worse, it's ground our project to a halt. We're dead in the water until we find out why it's happening and how to stop it. Those are two very big tasks, especially since we can't access the Lab anymore. And the worst-case scenario is the contaminant might eventually escape the lab module and enter the ship. I think you'll agree that if that ever happens it's curtains not only for our project but for us, too.

"But wait. It gets better."

Alice grinned at the eye rolls that greeted her comment. At least she had their attention.

"I've mapped out the cascading failure in the environmental controls and if nothing improves we'll have to evacuate the ship within 36 hours. It will simply be too hot to inhabit by then."

"We could always just open a door and let in the outside air," said Dmitri.

"That might help with some of the corridors, but every interior room including our personal quarters will still continue to heat up – there's simply not enough air transmission to help the sections that are farthest away from the outside access ports. Plus, as the temperature rises the ship's internal systems will start to fail. None of them were made to operate above a constant 200 degrees, which is where I estimate the temperature is heading within three days."

"So one of two things will probably kill us," said Vedana thoughtfully. "Either we roast to death or, when Lab 3's integrity fails, we freeze to death. And while we wait for the ship to freeze solid or to essentially melt in a cascading series of system failures, our only option is to evacuate to the surface, which is somewhere around eleven degrees below zero. Celsius."

"Right. I think that sums it up."

Claude shook his head slowly. His natural inclination toward collecting mountains of data on any problem, and then studying that data to death, was preventing him from accepting Alice's hastily-concluded assumptions.

"How sure are you that the seal on Lab 3 will fail? The labs were constructed with precisely this purpose in mind."

Before Alice could answer Dmitri broke in. "I'll take this one, Alice."

"I think Alice is right about this one." Dmitri was the only one of their team who had actually been working hands-on at the lab module. "I can't use the waldoes anymore because the servos and the hydraulics are frozen solid. The silicon seals on the door are actually cracking from the cold. Inside the module the temperature has already dropped below -100 Celsius.

"Ah, that's about -150 in Fahrenheit, Alice," he added with an evil grin. She showed him her finger. Pretending not to notice, he picked up speaking where he'd left off.

"The labs were designed to maintain their integrity under normal conditions. There was never any expectation that the interior of the labs themselves would be subjected to temperature extremes. What's more, the temperature differential between the interior of the ship and inside the lab is putting enormous stresses on the unit. A breach is almost inevitable – I myself had estimated about six days max before Lab 3 is compromised. It may be much sooner."

"Could we shut down the fusion reactor to stop the progression of heat within the ship?" asked Claude.

"And turn the entire ship into a dark, inert lump of steel and ceramic, with no life support or any other services?" replied Alice testily. "Sure. That might work."

"Sarcasm isn't helpful, Alice," said Claude reproachfully.

Alice sighed and sunk down into a chair. "You're right, and I'm sorry for being glib, Claude. But I'm starting to feel overwhelmed."

But almost immediately Alice perked up in her chair and said, "But all hope is not lost. I think I might have the beginnings of a plan to save our butts."

If she had had their attention before, she absolutely owned it now.

"It's actually a pretty simple solution: We need to kill the runaway experiment in Lab 3, stop the ship's overheating problem, and then entice our enemy to strike at us again, but this time we'll be waiting and we'll capture them, discover how they've sabotaged our project, and eliminate their interference."

"Oh, is that all," said Vedana.

Alice shot her an evil glance but was immediately disarmed as Vedana gave her the sexiest, dirtiest wink she'd ever seen. Alice actually blushed, and then quickly composed herself.

"The way I see it, we've been complicating our situation by depending on technology and science to find a solution. I want to go Old School.

"We need to shut down the experiment without acknowledging that we can't control it. Simple. We set fire to the lab.

"To the whole module, in fact. There are enough flammable liquids in there to provide a spectacular blaze, and we can set them off with a simple electrical pulse that we can send through the ceramic flooring panels."

"The ship's ceramics don't conduct electricity, Alice," said Claude.

"These do. The lab modules are independent and self-contained, so they don't share life support or environmental control systems with the rest of the ship. The ceramic panels in the floor were designed to act as heating elements to provide radiant heating to the lab. They are excellent electrical conductors and we should have no trouble at all in shorting them out and inducing an arc big enough to ignite the chemicals. I just hope we don't explode the whole shebang and blow a hole in the side of the ship."

"What about the fire suppression measures?" asked Claude.

Alice cackled. "That's the best part! The labs use Halon gas to suffocate any fire, but we vented all the Halon from Lab 3 when we started the project because we didn't want an accidental discharge of Halon to interfere with the compound's freezing reaction, since Halon is freeze resistant. Lab 3 no longer has any fire suppression measures in place. It's almost as if we planned this from the start!"

Alice was gratified to hear a chorus of grunts in assent. In her experience, that was high praise coming from a group of scientists.

Alice turned her back to them and quickly studied the whiteboard to check her next step.

"OK, I think when you hear this next part you're going to get excited. I downloaded a spec sheet on this ship from the computer banks and I found something interesting."

She paused to take a drink of water, and Claude and Dmitri followed suit. With the heat at its current levels they were all drinking and sweating multiple quarts of water each day. Only Vedana remained motionless, waiting for Alice to continue.

"We know that our enemy has tampered with the environmental controls. They've probably inserted malicious code into the system and it doesn't surprise me that none of the room-temperature-IQ techs who signed on to this doomed enterprise can properly debug the system.

"BUT, we don't need to debug the system. The ship will do it for us!

"Both the system's primary code and a basic version of one other critical system – life support – are hard-coded right into the main computer's BIOS. Any catastrophic event, such as an asteroid collision, a hull breach, or… *a fire*… will force the system to rescan all ship diagnostics and reboot and reset any individual systems where the readings are outside a predetermined set of parameters. If the corrupted system includes life support the computer will purge the existing code and load the basic version right from the BIOS.

"So far we've been told the life support backup systems must also be corrupted because the malfunction continues, but whoever corrupted the primary and backup versions of the program has no access to the hard-coded version. The fire we start will trick the main computer into reloading that original code and no one can prevent it. Problem *solved*."

Alice looked triumphant, and she deservedly sat down and took a deep breath.

Claude, analytical as ever, contemplated Alice's plan and then said, "Wouldn't it be better to run this past the Captain before we start setting fires on his ship?"

"No, most definitely, most assuredly not," answered Alice, with as much emphasis as she could inject into her voice. "For all we know it's the Captain who's behind all this. We can't trust anyone but the people in this room."

"And Manuel," added Vedana.

"And Manuel," agreed Alice. "Say, what do you suppose is keeping him? I left a note on his desk. He should have been here by now."

CHAPTER XII

MANUEL SPUN the large wheel mounted on the center of the pressure door and watched the long locking bolts slowly draw back. With a slight puff and a sigh the door released its seal.

Taking a deep breath, he slowly pulled the door open and gasped as the rush of outside air engulfed him. The sensation of being hit with subzero wind after he had been locked for days in this ginormous sauna was akin to being slapped in the face.

At least he was dressed for it. If anyone on the ship had come across him as he made his way from his quarters to the exit door they might have thought he had gone crazy from the heat. He wore thermal sweatpants and a long-sleeved sweatshirt, and he carried a small woolen skullcap. He was ready for the chill winds outside and he stepped through the portal and didn't bother to pull the door shut behind him.

Outside contaminants entering the ship were the least of their problems now. Besides, the air outside had been studied to death when this planet had first been claimed; it was remarkably similar to Earth's, and the few foreign agents it did include were all completely benign, and in fact had already been discovered and catalogued on dozens of other worlds. It seems the universe offered fewer surprises than mankind had expected. Life must evolve pretty consistently throughout the galaxy.

The thought was simultaneously both comforting and unsettling. He wondered when – or if – humans would encounter others like themselves, on one of the millions of far-flung planets scattered throughout the galaxy. So far, though, they were unique. The only sentient, self-aware species across thousands of light years. How incredible was *that?*

The starship they had flown to this planet had been specifically designed to land planetside and to act as a stationary base; when it landed internal gyroscopic stabilizers helped the ship settle into a perfectly level orientation as the intense heat captured by the superstructure during entry melted a perfect cradle into the planet's surface. To a casual observer from a distance it would appear uncannily similar to a beached ship stranded on a sandbar.

In fact, it was laid out not so differently from a traditional ocean liner, with decks, gangways and open landing areas. Manuel had chosen Deck 9 because it featured an open deck that wrapped entirely around the ship. It would serve perfectly as a running track, and he set off on a quick jog before the cold could start to really bite into him.

Large puffy streams of condensed air burst from his mouth as he trotted along the deck. He looked to his side at the planetscape stretching off into the distance, and saw that the surface was about 30 meters below him. It was frozen solid, and thin tendrils of frost bled up the sides of the ship. *Better not slip and fall,* he thought. *There won't be any splash at the bottom — that surface looks hard as concrete.*

Manuel picked up his pace a bit and tried to breathe a bit deeper. After suffocating in that sweatbox for the last few weeks, it was a delight to feel the chill in the air.

He'd already run halfway around the ship and had come to a part where a bulkhead briefly bulged out into his path, probably to accommodate some internal system, and when he jogged a bit closer to the rail to move around the protrusion a crewman working about 50 meters away suddenly came into view.

He might have thought nothing of it except for the fact that when the fellow looked up and saw Manuel running toward him at top speed, he suddenly dropped his tools and took off in the opposite direction.

That can't be good, thought Manuel.

If he'd thought about it, Manuel might have acted differently; but in the moment, his instincts kicked in and he automatically picked up his speed and ran after the fellow.

Despite having already run halfway around the ship Manuel was nowhere near out of breath. He rapidly closed the distance between him and the fleeing crewman, who had not been prepared for a chase. Manuel saw him slip briefly on the deck but he quickly recovered and a minute later he disappeared out of sight as he passed behind another protrusion.

Manuel pushed to increase his speed a bit more. He would need to catch up to the fellow before they got to the access door that Manuel had left open. Right now his quarry couldn't escape into the ship because the time it took to unlatch any entry door would provide more than sufficient delay for Manuel to catch up to him. But if he made it to the portal that Manuel hadn't bothered closing he could easily jump inside and turn the tables by actually locking Manuel out.

Of course, the man couldn't know about the open door. If Manuel could catch up to him before they got there, there would be no escaping him.

Manuel ran at top speed down the deck and rounded the protrusion his target had disappeared behind, and almost immediately his foot skidded in front of him and he became airborne, sliding out of control and smashing at top speed into a cooling tower.

He was fortunate not to crash into the tower head first, instead impacting the barrier with his shoulder but tumbling badly in the process. He felt something snap in his ankle and he grimaced as a lance of pain shot through his body.

He came to a stop turned backwards and saw that the man he had been chasing had stopped behind the protrusion and had opened an insulated water faucet jutting out from a maintenance station. The spilled water had turned icy slick in the seconds after it had splashed onto the frigid decking, and had caught Manuel completely unawares.

The crewman was still there, still pressed against the bulkhead. He looked at Manuel laying on the deck and cursed to see that his pursuer was still conscious and, worst of all, was looking directly at him. He strode purposely over to Manuel, who still lay on the deck, now clutching his ankle, and withdrew a small vial from a zippered breast pocket on his coveralls.

He looked down at Manuel and said, "Sorry buddy. Nothing personal." And then he tugged the cap off the top of the vial and splashed the contents at Manuel's face.

As luck would have it, a sudden gust of wind whipping across the deck scattered most of the contents of the vial off to the side, but a few droplets still made it to Manuel, who had instinctively raised his arm to protect his face. He felt the drops splash onto his sleeve, and peripherally saw one drop fall down and darken into a little spot on his left foot which he had been cradling after snapping his ankle.

His assailant didn't wait to see the results of his attack, but instead quickly turned and ran back along the deck in the direction they had come from.

"I guess I'm lucky," muttered Manuel. "If that was some kind of acid, he missed me. Doesn't look like much damage was done."

It wasn't more than a few seconds, however, before his optimism turned to horror.

Before his eyes the darkened spots where the liquid had hit him suddenly turned deathly white, and then tiny, spidery tendrils rapidly started to spread out from each dot, building a frosty web of crystals that rapidly blossomed along his sleeve.

"Madre de Dios!" he shrieked. Manuel lapsed into Spanish usually only in times of great distress. This qualified.

Manuel recognised the freezing compound immediately and he frantically yanked at his sweatshirt and tore it from his body in a frenzy, being careful nonetheless not to let any part of its exterior touch him. He flung it off to the side – downwind – and immediately turned his attention to his running shoe which was also rapidly turning frosty white.

The heel of his shoe was so far uncontaminated and with a superhuman effort he grasped his shoe by the heel and yanked it off his foot. Despite still being laced up, the shoe pulled free but Manuel almost vomited from the shaft of pain that blossomed up from his shattered ankle. Still, a small price to pay to keep from being turned into a popsicle.

He flung the shoe away in the direction he had thrown his sweatshirt and collapsed back momentarily onto the deck. His ankle was sending lightning bolts of pain up his leg but Manuel knew he had to get up somehow and make it back into the ship. Shirtless as he now was, a few minutes in this weather would kill him just as surely as a bullet. He willed himself up and almost blacked out as the intense agony in his leg assaulted him with increased vigour.

He reached out and put a hand on the cooling tower to steady himself. The pain in his ankle wasn't abating and he was having trouble staying conscious.

It didn't make sense. Manuel had broken bones before and the pain hadn't been anywhere near this excruciating. He bent over and pulled up the leg of his sweatpants to see if any bones were actually poking out of his skin. What he saw almost stopped his heart on the spot.

Manuel's sprained ankle wasn't the source of his pain.

He cried out in terror as he discovered that one other dot of liquid had made it onto him, this one landing in the tiny space between the bottom of his sweatpants leg and the top of his sock.

Frantically he pulled the sweatpants leg up as high as he could above his calf. Already a thick web of icy tendrils wrapped his lower leg, and was visibly spreading higher even as he watched.

Panicking, he irrationally swatted at the infection swallowing his leg, only to realise that he had now spread it onto his hand as well.

"Gaaah," he croaked. Futilely he flung himself off the cooling tower and tried to hobble across the deck but it was already too late. He couldn't so much as take a single step before he tumbled down face first onto the deck.

His left leg was now a useless chunk of frozen flesh and he grimaced as he felt his torso start to stiffen. He looked at his bare arm, splayed out before him on the deck. His hand was now icy white and thick ropes of frost snaked up his arm. Manuel felt the first few twinges of cold hit his neck, just before the world went black and he passed out of consciousness.

CHAPTER XIII

SIGURD SAT in his workspace and fretted.

He worried that the scientists were catching up to his plans. Left to their own devices they would surely figure out a solution to the obstacles he had engineered.

He couldn't wait for that to happen. He needed to hurry things along. And there remained only one means to do that.

When he had originally sabotaged the experiment in Lab 3 he had fortuitously thought to take a backup sample of the freezing compound. The main supply of the chemical mix was stored in Claude Boisset's office safe where Sigurd couldn't reach it, but in preparation for the controlled conditions test the scientists had left a small vial of the compound waiting in Lab 3. After he had altered the test supply he took a fractional amount of solution to use at a later date, if need be. There was no telling if he would ever be able to access another sample again and he wasn't going to waste the opportunity.

He didn't dare leave the sample in his own quarters, or anywhere else in the ship for that matter, as he was simply terrified of it. He had seen with his own eyes how quickly even a tiny amount could overwhelm an area and spread its icy poison onto anything it encountered.

His best option had been to stash the small vial on the outside of the ship. This was actually the best plan of action, he mused, since there was never any need for any personnel to access the exterior. He would have complete privacy outside, which was a lot more than you could say for life inside a starship.

And now he had determined that the best way to stop the scientists cold – *so to speak, heh heh* – was to release the compound into the main scientific section. They wouldn't be solving any problems if their desks, monitors and entire offices were coated in a thick sheet of ice.

Of course, it would inevitably necessitate the evacuation of the ship, but Sigurd had already accepted that fate. As far as he was concerned, they would either all die quite soon or be stranded here permanently on this wretched joke of a planet. Given the choice, he would prefer the former.

Consequently, a few minutes later he found himself sneaking along the deck on the ship's exterior, screwdriver in hand, to retrieve his vial of death that he had tucked away behind a maintenance panel.

It was a quick operation – a couple of screws, a quick grab of the vial, which he sealed into his breast pocket, and *snap!* The panel was back in place.

It was just then that he looked up and saw the man racing toward him from up the deck. He recognised him immediately as one of the scientists running the experiment. And unfortunately, it was the one guy who looked like he was in top shape. Sigurd wasn't sure he could take the man in a fair fight.

How was I spotted? he screamed in his mind. *This is catastrophic!*

Without pausing to think, he dropped his screwdriver and spun off down the deck at top speed away from the man who was bearing down on him at a breakneck pace.

Pumped with adrenalin and panic, Sigurd made good time in the first couple of minutes of their chase, but his pursuer was definitely catching up and Sigurd was starting to crash. Worse, there was nowhere to escape to. Any entry port Sigurd might try to disappear into would take precious seconds to open, and the other guy would surely catch up to him before he could gain access.

Well, Sigurd suspected he would lose against this man in a fair fight, but who said he had to fight fair?

In his paranoia he had thoroughly inspected the ship's decks just after they had landed planetside; knowing the lay of the land could offer a person a significant advantage, and Sigurd believed in being prepared.

He racked his brain as he ran, thinking frantically what sort of implements, tools, or ship's equipment he might be able to access to overcome his adversary. As he ran he briefly lost his footing on the slick deck and immediately an idea flashed into his head. And as luck would have it, they were coming up on the perfect spot for his little plan to be enacted.

As he dashed around a protrusion and located the maintenance faucet he knew was there, Sigurd could hear the other man's footfalls pounding on the deck. They sounded even more rapid, and Sigurd figured the guy was really putting on the gas in a desperate attempt to catch up. Perfect. Exactly what he needed.

The water gushed out of the faucet immediately and Sigurd took his boot and kicked as much of it as he could closer to the transitway before tucking himself behind the protrusion in the bulkhead and awaiting his pursuer's arrival.

When the fellow hit the patch of icy water the result was even more spectacular than Sigurd had expected. His foot shot out explosively beneath him and he actually sailed through the air for a few feet before he came to a sudden and obviously painful stop against a cooling tower rising from the deck.

Sigurd was dismayed to see that his adversary hadn't knocked himself out. Worse, he was staring directly at him.

He reflected that, true, they were all probably going to die here, but he had a hard time actually killing another human being.

In all the death and destruction he had caused in his life with all his various eco-terrorist activities, he had never personally taken another man's life face to face. Like the pilot who blithely carpet-bombs whole villages from the safety of his jet at 30,000 feet of separation from his victims, but who could never actually bludgeon another person to death with his own hands, Sigurd recoiled from the thought of personally and directly snuffing out another man's life.

And yet, here it was. The fellow was looking directly at him. His cover was blown at precisely the most delicate point in his mission.

Sighing, and recognising that he simply had no other choice, Sigurd reached down into his pocket and pulled out the vial.

Sort of like shooting an unarmed man, he thought, but he had no desire to risk a struggle with this man, injured or no.

He tried to make it quick. He mumbled an apology and then splashed the vial into the man's face and turned away as quickly as he could. He didn't want to see what he had done. He actually felt sick.

Sigurd trotted back up the deck and retrieved his screwdriver and then headed back inside the ship. *Now I'm* really *screwed,* he thought. *How am I ever going to get my hands on more of the compound?*

This was turning into a *really* shitty day.

CHAPTER XIV

AS THE DAY'S light was slowly swallowed by the inky black of night, from the frozen, prone figure stretched out on Deck 9 thick ropy streams of ice methodically crawled out and began to engulf the ship's surface. Frigid gusts of wind swept up from the barren plain below and peppered the deck with a harsh mixture of sand and snow and atmospheric grit.

The spreading ice continued its relentless march across the deck and began a slow climb up the sides of the bulkheads. As the first flecks of snow began to fall from the sky, spiderwebs of frost trickled up and then across the portholes on Deck 9's interior promenade. By the time darkness had completely enveloped the ship, a thick sheet of ice lay across several hundred meters of Deck 9.

CHAPTER XV

DESPITE THEIR best efforts, it took seemingly forever for the four scientists to hammer out all the details of their plan before they were comfortable with it. By then they were all tired and hungry, and they headed as a group down to the commissary for a late supper. Alice cautioned them all not to mention a word about their plans anywhere on the ship where prying eyes – or ears – might be present.

It was a blessing, of sorts, that they were forced to spend an hour together talking about everything except work. Alice kept the group in stitches relating a seemingly endless string of anecdotes about her prior work assignments.

It seemed to Vedana that the little redhead had worked on half the known worlds in the galaxy. She wondered just how old Alice was; she'd never asked her, but had always assumed that she was in her early 30's, at most. Her youthful vigour and irrepressible humour gave her an ageless quality that rendered her actual calendar age meaningless, as far as Vedana was concerned. She liked the feisty little minx and realised she was falling hard.

Dmitri proved to be the perfect straight man for Alice, and kept leading her into one ribald recollection after another. The two of them had worked together for the last few years and the affection they shared for each other was clear.

Claude, like Vedana, mostly sat back with an amused smile on his face as he observed the two scientists bantering with each other. Claude was one of those steady, "anchor" type presences that every successful team needed, reflected Vedana. She had known him only a few months but had been flattered by the confidence he had shown in her judgment and intelligence.

Dmitri was Claude's partner, but Vedana had quickly become his safety backup. Claude had taken to running almost every decision past Vedana before he acted on it. And when she had objections he took them seriously.

Vedana was supremely comfortable with this tight-knit little group of her peers and the only thing she felt was lacking right now was Manuel. *I wonder where he's gotten to*, she wondered. *Could something bad have happened to him?*

She hoped that her concern was misplaced, though, and that the attractive Spaniard was merely off catching some well-deserved rest. The last few weeks had been hard on everybody and the stress was threatening to build up to toxic levels. And after Alice's meeting paranoia levels were rising dangerously high.

The thought made Vedana turn her attention to Alice. She watched the chattering firecracker of a scientist rattling off names and dates and harking back to misadventures on some far off planet, and she felt a warm wave of emotion rush through her. She was supremely grateful to be entering into a relationship with her emotive little friend. And a delicious tingle in her nether regions reminded her that the benefits of a relationship with Alice went far beyond those of an intellectually stimulating nature.

Before long, the two men both rose and excused themselves. Claude was probably heading back to his office to study some more data sets, mused Vedana, but she wouldn't be surprised if Dmitri were heading to the Officer's Bar on Deck 6. All the scientists were welcome there but only Dmitri really got along well with the hard-bitten spacers that patronized the place.

Which left her sitting here, all alone once again, with Alice.

Neither woman said anything for a moment, and Alice dipped her chin and looked up at Vedana through her eyelashes, a mischievous smile playing across her lips.

I wonder if she's aware how coquettish she's being right now, wondered Vedana. *Does she do that on purpose, or is it just natural…?*

"Sooooo…" said Alice, as Vedana gazed at her. "Um, whaddaya wanna do now, hon?"

Vedana barked out a laugh and grabbed the other woman behind her neck and pulled her face close to her own.

"I have an idea," she said, as Alice, lower lip gently gripped between her teeth, stared deeply into her eyes. "Why don't we go back to your quarters and try to remember where we left off earlier today on that couch over there in the corner?"

Anyone watching the two women would have at that point been startled to see how quickly they left their table to disappear out the door and down the corridor.

CHAPTER XVI

SIGHING HEAVILY, Alice collapsed onto her couch, flopping backward and splaying her legs out before her.

"Fuuuuuck, it's so hot !" she moaned. The display on the wall by the door read 121 degrees.

Vedana laughed heartily. "I can feel it on my face," she said. "But the rest of me is as cool as a cucumber. This suit is worth its weight in gold!"

Alice eyed Vedana, who had shucked her lab coat and stood in front of the little redhead chuckling at her misery.

"Well I hate to break it to you, hon, but that suit's coming off as soon as I can arrange it, so you'd better prepare yourself to step into this sauna."

"Mmmmmm," Vedana replied, sinking to her knees between Alice's open legs and bringing her face up to hers.

"You know," said Alice, "It occurs to me that we haven't even kissed each other yet."

"I've been saving that," answered Vedana. "It's my favourite part. I wanted it to be just right."

Alice blushed, flattered at the affection and desire Vedana was showing her.

Vedana collapsed down onto the couch beside Alice. She wrapped her arm around the other woman's neck and said softly, "You're beautiful." And she pulled tightly against Alice and brought her mouth down to hers and kissed her deeply.

It was one of those kisses where each person loses themselves for a moment, deep in the intensity of their lover's warmth and closeness and pure intimacy of contact. They felt each other breathing, they luxuriated in the sensation of each other's mouth, and for one brief moment they both felt as though they were actually a part of the other person.

When they finally broke the kiss Alice simply melted into Vedana's arms. Normally, she was the dominant partner in any relationship but for the first time she was thrilled to cede control to her mate. At that moment, she couldn't have asked for more than to let Vedana do with her as she would, and to give herself completely to this sensual European temptress.

They lay together like that for a moment before Alice suddenly jerked and said, "Hey! Why should I be the only one sitting here drenched in sweat while you're still wrapped from head to ankle in that clothing?"

"Well, you can hardly call this clothing, now can you? I constantly feel like I'm walking around naked as a jaybird when I'm wearing this outfit. Normally I would never dare to parade around like this, but I don't often have to work in an oven. Desperate times, desperate measures, right?"

"It *is* a pretty appealing sight, I must admit," said Alice, running her hand along Vedana's stomach. "When we were in the commissary this afternoon I felt if I closed my eyes I could believe that you were actually naked. There aren't even any seams or buttons or zippers. How do you take it off?"

By way of explanation Vedana stood and grasped her cuff with her opposite hand and pulled her arm up and out of the outfit, repeated the process on her opposite arm, then pulled her entire outfit down her body and off her ankles.

"See? Super super stretchy. And the only part of me that's even slightly damp are these little spaces here right below and between my boobs, where the suit doesn't quite maintain contact with my skin."

Alice didn't respond and Vedana looked up at her quizzically, but noticed the expression on Alice's face.

With the removal of the bright white garment Vedana's lithe, caramel-coloured body, glorious and sexy in its nakedness, was breathtaking in its perfection. Alice had thought that the bodysuit left nothing to the imagination but as she drank in the sight of Vedana's nicely muscled, toned body revealed in beautiful smoky hues, she realised she hadn't even begun to appreciate the intense animal sexuality of her new lover.

"Oh. My. Ghod." said Alice.

"My thoughts exactly," replied Vedana, leaning forward to pull Alice's shorts off. "Well, that and *'Good Grief it's hot in here!'* How do you people live in these conditions?"

CHAPTER XVII

SO I'VE BEEN thinking," began Vedana, laying back in a pool of sweat on Alice's kitchen floor.

Both women had decamped to the kitchen in search of cool drinks, and they lay there on their backs in front of the open refrigerator door, which bled a stream of chilled air out and over their sweaty naked bodies.

"Mm-hmm," answered Alice dreamily. She kept unconsciously reaching out to caress Vedana's tummy with her hand, but would immediately withdraw it as she felt their clammy contact. Each time she did so Vedana chuckled, and mentally counted the seconds until Alice would once again instinctively reach out to touch her, and the cycle would begin again.

"You haven't figured out how to trap our prey yet, have you?"

Alice's eyes snapped back into focus as her mind suddenly jumped to their predicament.

"No. I keep thinking of ideas but none are practical. Why?"

"Because I've got one. Like you said, let's keep it simple and Old School.

"Our enemy can't realise yet that we've decided to set a trap, so let's draw them in just as we did the first time they hit us, only we didn't know then that we were targets."

"I'm not sure I follow. What do you have in mind?"

"Well, they messed with our first experiment, right? And they were spectacularly successful. So tomorrow after we incinerate Lab 3, let's act as though we're still stuck on the same track, and set up an identical experiment in one of the other lab modules.

There's an excellent chance our adversaries will conclude we've learned nothing and will try to sabotage the new experiment exactly as they did last week.

"We'll set a trap and if we're lucky not only will we catch the sons of bitches red-handed, we'll learn exactly how they're disrupting the compound. We can coat the lab with a UV powder and surreptitiously check for intruders every hour or so, and then track them back to their evil lair."

Alice sat up, eyes gleaming. "Vedana, that's an excellent idea – it's so simple and yet devilishly clever! I can't believe I didn't think of that myself!"

"Thank you so much," said Vedana, dryly.

Alice swatted her on the arm. "Oh shut up. You know what I mean."

She leaned over and planted a wet kiss on Vedana's mouth. "I knew I loved you for more than just your body."

CHAPTER XVIII

ALICE LAY BACK in the darkness, watching the various little lights, sensors, LEDs and diagnostics panels twinkling away around her.

It had been Vedana's idea to move into Lab 2. After Alice had casually mentioned during their meeting that the lab modules had independent life support systems she peripherally realised that they offered a handy respite from the oppressive heat engulfing the ship.

But only once she had shucked her bodysuit in Alice's quarters and the heat hit her with full force did the thoughts that had slumbered in the periphery of her brain suddenly become predominant. It didn't take any convincing at all to make Alice quickly gather up their clothes and two sleep pads and to all but run over to the lab module. They didn't even bother getting dressed. They simply trotted through the darkened deserted corridors naked as the day they were born and punched in the entry code to open the lab door.

As soon as they entered the module they both groaned in delight at the wave of cool air that washed over them.

They threw down their sleep pads in a clear space on the far side of the lab and collapsed in a heap. It wasn't more than five minutes, however, before they both developed restless hands, and found themselves greedily caressing each other in a steadily intensifying embrace.

Vedana had been with both men and women before, of course, but Alice exhibited a level of sexual intensity Vedana had never previously encountered.

It wasn't merely that the woman was insatiable. It was the raw passion she expressed, as though she had been waiting years for this very moment and now was releasing every ounce of energy and pure lust that she had been storing up all that time.

Vedana couldn't help but comment on it, and Alice struggled to put her response into words.

"It's more than just the physical sensations. It's… symbolic, I guess. I'm not like this with everyone, you know. For me sex is often akin to just scratching an itch, and there's usually a lot less emotion involved than you might expect.

"But I feel differently about you. We've spent the last four months locked up together in this tin can and almost from the moment I met you I've felt a closeness that I haven't felt before. I've heard it called *simpatico*, but I'd never experienced it firsthand.

"I enjoy your company almost as much when we're just sitting around gabbing as I do when we're involved in an intimate embrace. I sense a rare emotional connection with you that's been so elusive with most of my partners.

"And then when I can give absolutely all of myself to you and surrender to your touch it's as though you're taking ownership of me, possessing me…. It's hard to explain. I think I derive my greatest thrill from being totally yours. It's a tangible display of my absolute devotion to you."

"Wow," whispered Vedana. "I don't think anyone's ever said something like that to me before."

"Well, get used to it, honey. I'm not going anywhere. And you're not getting away."

Alice collapsed down onto the sleep mat beside Vedana and lay there quietly, listening to the other woman's breathing.

After a moment, Vedana, still staring straight up in the darkness, said quietly, "And just imagine how good it will be when we get to know what each other really likes…."

Both women giggled and, snuggling up against each other in the cool air, drifted off to sleep.

CHAPTER XIX

VEDANA WAS DREAMING.

She was trapped in a lab, and the ice was growing all around her. Outside the lab she could see all her colleagues through the module's glass wall, but they seemed blissfully unaware of her or her predicament. She shouted and waved, but not one of them even so much as glanced in her direction.

Frantically, she picked up a hammer and smacked it against the glass, but all she could manage was a pathetic series of little taps.

Tap tap tap! Tap tap tap! And *still* no one looked over at her!

Tap tap tap!

Tap tap tap!

Vedana opened her eyes. She tried to focus on her surroundings. *Tap tap tap!*

She was awake now – why was she still hear— OH NO!

In horror, Vedana snapped her head around and looked at the lab's glass wall, where on the other side Claude and Dmitri were frantically tapping on the glass trying to rouse her.

She and Alice were still splayed out on the lab's floor in glorious, obscene nudity, their tangled limbs telling the tale of last night's debauchery more eloquently than the most explicit sex vid ever could have.

They had locked themselves inside the lab for privacy's sake, which now seemed a cruel, ludicrous joke.

"Alice Alice Alice wake up Alice!" She violently shook the sleeping redhead, who woke up much as Vedana had, slowly and dreamily.

"Hey babe," slurred Alice through sleepy eyes.

"Alice you need to wake up NOW," said Vedana with quiet urgency. "I think that damage to our professional reputations that we spoke of earlier might have arrived."

Alice looked up at the two scientists impatiently gesticulating on the other side of the glass wall and shrieked.

It was a little late of course, but Claude and Dmitri turned away to afford the two women a modicum of privacy as they hastily clothed themselves before rushing over to unlock the lab door.

When Alice and Vedana emerged from the lab Claude looked a little uncomfortable but Dmitri was in stitches.

"Well I see *someone* had a good night," he began, but Alice cut him off with a vicious glare.

"Don't start, Dmitri. We all remember what happened on Montezuma's Moon when you tried Gamedian brandy for the first time."

Dmitri suddenly turned bright red and his smile vanished.

"You said you'd never mention that again –"

"Yeah, well, desperate times, etc, right?"

"Besides," mumbled Dmitri grumpily, "That judge really should have been satisfied with just issuing a warning…."

Alice leaned forward and gave him a quick peck on the cheek.

"I'm sure if you and Claude had thought of camping out in one of the lab modules you'd have done so too," she added.

"Well, maybe not exactly the way you did…" murmured Claude.

"Um…" began Dmitri, awkwardly, "Ah, I don't know exactly how to phrase this, but did Manuel, that is, was Manuel also in there… did he –"

Vedana put Dmitri out of his misery by quickly answering, "No, it's just us two. Don't tell me Manny is still missing?"

"Unhappily, yes," said Claude. "When we couldn't find any of you in your quarters Dmitri and I started to panic, and then when we located you here we briefly hoped that all three of you…."

He let the thought drift off.

"This is bad," said Alice. "I knew we were all in danger, but this ups the ante quite a bit. I hadn't thought our personal safety was at risk."

"Aren't you rushing to conclusions?" asked Claude.

"Come on, Claude," said Alice. "What other explanation can you come up with for one of our team members suddenly disappearing? Do you think he caught a bus back home maybe?"

Silence settled on the little group as the gravity of the situation impressed itself on them.

Vedana broke the silence by snapping them all back to attention.

"Look, it sucks that Manny's missing and we'll deal with that real soon, but first we've got to get our plan going." She looked over at a wall panel. "Holy crap! Does that really say '131'?"

The perspiration dripping off Claude's forehead and soaking his t-shirt was all the confirmation she needed.

"We have no time to waste, guys," said Vedana. "Dmitri, lead the way. Time to get to work on Lab 3."

It had been days since any of the scientists except Dmitri had visited Lab 3. Essentially, they were all quite scared of it and subconsciously avoided it. For once, their scientific curiosity had taken second place to their survival instincts. Even Claude had remained distant and checked all the diagnostics remotely from his office.

When they turned the corner and Lab 3 came into view there was a collective gasp.

The lab's large, floor-to-ceiling glass wall was crisscrossed with spiderwebs of frost. The only reason it hadn't iced over completely must have been the superheated air from the ship that constantly washed over it.

Inside, the lab looked like a post-apocalyptic vision from an abandoned ice planet. Huge cascades of ice hung off the counters and oozed from the shelving units. The area where the tomato plant experiment had been located was now nothing more than a gigantic snow bank, glimmering and glistening in the reflected light from the corridor.

Every other surface in the lab module was iced over and dripping with what looked like snow.

"It's freezing the moisture in the air," said Dmitri quietly. "And the carbon dioxide. In a few hours it will chill the nitrogen in the air to the point where it will actually liquefy, and about two hours after that, solidify."

"Is there still enough oxygen left to supply a fire?" asked Alice quietly. "I see three large oxygen tanks over there in the corner, but they're probably frozen, too."

"Well, oxygen would be the last gas to freeze, but we're not going to be burning oxygen," replied Dmitri. "You see those two canisters on the floor over there? The ones marked "RDX" and "AA"?

"Those are canisters of nitrogen explosives – the second one, the Aziroazide azide, that's one of the most explosive compounds known to man, and the RDX is a close second. They're composed of nitrogen-nitrogen bonds instead of oxygen atoms. They're both highly unstable and incredibly dangerous."

"And they're in our lab," said Vedana quietly.

"Well, as long as you treat the canisters with respect you don't need to worry. I wouldn't go chucking them down a flight of stairs or rolling them down the halls, though."

"Aren't those the explosives we used to blast a drill hole for the first test?" asked Claude.

"The very same. And you'll recall the tiny amount we used and the size of the crater that resulted."

"God, Dmitri," said Alice, running her hand through her hair in approaching panic, "I'm thinking we might want to reconsider this plan. We don't want to demolish half the ship. We need it to get home, remember?"

"Already thought of that, Alice," said Dmitri. "You can still just make out the pressure gauge readings on both tanks. They're both almost empty. It's a security precaution. Carrying a full tank of those things would be like carting around a nuclear bomb. By keeping each tank almost empty we can reduce our risk to killing maybe just the people in the lab if one were to suddenly detonate by accident."

"How comforting," mumbled Vedana, reflecting on how many times she had worked in that lab mere inches away from those deadly tubes.

"Now, nitrogen isn't flammable, but you'll notice the cabinets marked in red, well, you can't see them anymore because they're covered in ice, but they're there at the bottom. Those are the fireproof cabinets where we store our most flammable lab chemicals, Benzene, Cyclohexane, Ethanol, you get the idea.

The explosion should be powerful enough to destroy the cabinet and ignite the chemicals. The fire will burn hotter than the deepest pits of Hell, for at least twenty minutes by my estimation. That should be enough to completely and totally incinerate every last molecule of the freezing compound. And to trip the ship's emergency sensors."

"That sounds great, Dmitri, except for one little wrinkle," said Alice. "That's gonna be a powerful explosion, no matter how you cut it. And the way I see it, the immediate result will be a corridor full of shattered glass and highly dangerous freezing agents which will probably be aerosolized and dispersed throughout this entire deck, if not the whole ship. I wanted a fire, not an explosion. This glass wall will never stand a chance."

"That would be true if this were normal glass," answered Dmitri, "But don't forget these labs have been engineered to be virtually indestructible and specifically reinforced to contain explosions. This is not normal glass. It's a metallic glass that's both stronger and tougher than steel – than any other material known to man, in fact – and its molecular structure is amorphous, not crystalline. It is virtually impervious to fracturing. On Earth we use it to line nuclear reactors to avoid catastrophic failures.

"It's actually part of the ship's hull. When we mount the labs, we just seal them to the glass wall from the outside.

"And you should be especially proud of it, Alice, considering that it was your fellow countrymen, a group of scientists at CalTech, who invented it. The rest of the ship could disintegrate in a massive fusion reactor explosion and I wouldn't be surprised if this sheet of glass remained unscratched."

"But then won't the explosion blow the lab right off the ship?" asked Vedana.

"No, because we attach it with an epoxy that physically rearranges the atoms in the two surfaces and weaves them together on a molecular level. The resulting bond is actually stronger than either original material. Each square centimeter of the bonded material can resist approximately 3,000 tons of pressure. This lab isn't going *anywhere*."

"OK. Any other questions? No? Then someone come help me lug over the portable generator from my office and we can get to work burning this sucker down."

CHAPTER XX

THERE **WAS NOTHING** "portable" about Dmitri's generator, thought Vedana, as she struggled to drag the hulking beast down the corridor. She looked over at Dmitri and couldn't help but chuckle as she watched rivulets of perspiration stream down his face. This would have been a bear of a job in the best of conditions, but performing it in this oven of a ship rendered it simply torturous. Thank God she had her heat suit, although even her suit's systems were having trouble keeping up with the constantly increasing temperature. She could feel the warm air around her and she wondered at what temperature the suit would just shut down. She sure didn't want to find out anytime soon.

Claude and Alice were busy stringing a long thick electrical cable down the corridor. They had exposed one end and wedged it against the base of the lab door and were counting on the proximity to the ceramic tiles inside the room to allow the current to jump the threshold. They pulled the other end of the electrical cable over to the far end of the corridor leading to the lab module. They wanted to stay within sight of the lab, but no one was anxious to be within blast range of the module when they set it off, magic glass be damned.

The team made quick work of hooking up the cable and checking the setup and the final connection with the module's door. This was work they were good at, and they were happy to finally have something useful to do.

When the time came to set it off it was almost anticlimactic. Claude did the honours and pushed the button while the rest of them hunched down with their fingers in their ears.

Nothing.

He pushed it again.

Still nothing.

"Maybe you're not using enough juice, Claude," said Dmitri, and he cranked up the voltage regulator dial to the top.

"Try it now."

They were almost knocked onto their backsides by the bright flash that burst from the room as the ceramic tiles overloaded and spit out a lightning bolt of electricity that arced up from the floor. That was followed almost immediately by one of the loudest explosions any of them had ever heard, as the entire lab module virtually leapt in place. The entire ship shook as though it had just been rammed broadside at high speed by another starship.

Credit the original lab designers with doing at least one thing really well, thought Alice, as she saw the massive explosion blossom and then subside, almost simultaneously accompanied by a tremendous burst of flame as the chemicals in the fire cabinet ignited, which burned all the more intensely since the three oxygen tanks had immediately exploded and emptied their contents into the inferno. But the module's integrity held. The glass wall was blackened but apparently unharmed, without so much as a hairline fracture.

Immediately, ear-splitting klaxons started wailing throughout the ship as the main computer detected what it must have interpreted as a massive bomb detonating off the starboard hull. Inside the corridor where the science team huddled, Halon gas started to flood from the overhead vents. The ship thought this whole section was on fire and the fire suppression measures kicked in.

"Ack! Halon!" shouted Alice. "My God, won't this suck all the oxygen out of the air and suffocate us?" She grabbed Vedana's hand and pulled her along as she began to run down the corridor.

"Don't worry, Alice," called Dmitri after them. "That won't happen, but we do need to get out of here – we shouldn't inhale this stuff if we can avoid it. Come on, Claude!"

And through the rapidly descending cloud of gas the four scientists ran down the corridor and all but leapt into the next section of the ship, where they collapsed onto the decking, puffing and gasping for air, but otherwise unharmed.

CHAPTER XXI

CAPTAIN VAN **D**EEP leaned over the diagnostics display and studied the array of readouts.

He was peering at one particular gauge whose needle was planted firmly in the red when a large drop of perspiration dripped off his forehead and splashed down onto the display.

He looked up in exasperation. The Bridge was all but deserted, with only himself and one lonely Ensign on duty to monitor the ship's ongoing functions. He had released all the other Bridge personnel from their duties so they could do whatever they needed to cope with the intolerable heat.

The sailors shared a common aversion to exiting the confines of the ship even though they could have found brief respite from the oppressive heat by visiting one of the outdoor decks. One of the crew had gotten deathly sick just after they'd landed, and despite the Medical Officer's diagnosis that the man was suffering from a contagion picked up months earlier on a completely different planet, the crew were convinced the planet's air was toxic and infested with viral agents. They avoided the airlocks and outer access doors like… well, like the plague.

The Captain had no such concerns but he was stuck here on the Bridge, where even though the ship was stationary there were still duties to be performed and equipment to be monitored.

He looked back down at his console and reflected that he was lucky not to be colour-blind, because if he were unable to see the colour red his display panel would probably look quite blank. Almost every diagnostic readout was flashing red, needles were all pointing into the red, and every bar graph had moved into the red.

One by one, as the ship's internal heat climbed above maximum operating tolerances, all of the ship's systems were threatening to fail or to automatically shut down.

Certain sections were significantly hotter than others, probably owing to the nature of the equipment in their immediate vicinities. With a grimace van Deep noted that the Bridge, perversely, was one of those areas, boasting a temperature several degrees hotter than the rest of the Deck.

He sank back into his command chair and reached for his coffee. Thank God his Ensign was still up to the task.

It was just as he was raising the cup of hot java to his lips that the entire ship bucked and rocked violently in a massive wrenching shudder. A gigantic splash of boiling hot coffee sloshed over the edge of his cup and scalded his chest right though his uniform.

"Good God! What was that?!" he exclaimed at the hapless Ensign, who had almost tumbled off his seat.

"I think an explosion of some sort may have detonated on board, Sir," said the Ensign, frantically scanning his readouts. "Looks like it might have come from the science modules mounted on the starboard hull, Sir."

Van Deep buried his head in his hands and cursed. *Those idiots better not have blown a hole in the side of my ship! Wouldn't that just be the icing on the cake!*

Klaxons started ringing throughout the ship as the fire control measures kicked in.

Captain van Deep sighed, stood up and smoothed out his soaked uniform. Drops of coffee dripped down off his shirt and jacket and splashed onto his shoes. *Oh well,* he thought as he prepared to go down and inspect the damage in person, *at least this will give the crew something to do….*

CHAPTER XXII

ALICE LAY BACK, stretched out her legs luxuriously and rested her heels on a shelf opposite her chair. Arching her back, she shook out her hair and let it dangle down behind her chair as she raised her hands above her face as though she were trying to reach the ceiling. A little mew of pleasure came from her lips.

Claude and Dmitri, splayed out on two other chairs in Claude's office, joined her in groaning in indulgent delight as the wave of frigid air from the wall vents washed over them. Only Vedana, who stood watching the trio with her hands on her hips and a wry smile on her face, was not stretched out like an overheated housecat.

"You three are pathetic," she said reproachfully. "Have you never felt air conditioning before?"

"Oh, hush up, Vedana," said Alice. "You're just pissed because you're no longer the only one on board not drenched in sweat."

Vedana had just returned from her quarters where she had gratefully stripped off her heat suit and replaced it with a normal set of clothing, including a modest chemise and a tight knee-length pencil skirt. Her only concession to her more perverse nature was the addition of a pair of thigh-high sheer white stockings and pointy white shoes with three-inch-high stiletto heels. These items, along with a pair of the tiniest lacy white panties she had, she wore for Alice, whom she aimed to keep in a constant state of sexual arousal for as long as she was able.

The results of their incendiary activities had unfolded exactly as Alice had predicted. Within minutes of the fire breaking out in Lab 3 the ship's computer had performed all the emergency procedures described in the manual, including a full purging of the faulty life support program code and the uploading of uncorrupted code from the hard-coded storage.

Literally within minutes the temperatures on board had started plunging, and barely one hour later the wall displays all read "73". Vedana did some quick math in her head and grunted approvingly. Excellent conditions for doing work.

"Well, if there's a downside to all of this," said Dmitri, continuing to stare up at the ceiling, "I think it has to be that we can't look forward to seeing Vedana walk around naked anymore."

"DMITRI!" exclaimed Vedana as the other three guffawed.

"Speak for yourself, Dmitri," murmured Alice, with an evil grin on her lips.

"And I, for one, will miss their choice of sleeping compartments," said Claude.

"Oh my God, Claude," said Vedana. "Not you, too?"

Their rollicking laughter was contagious, though, and Vedana couldn't help but chuckle along with them.

Vedana begrudgingly admitted to herself that she would also miss the opportunity to indulge her exhibitionist tendencies.

Her initial modest reluctance to expose herself to her shipmates had quickly dissipated in the first few days that she'd worn her suit on board, and very quickly she had discovered that she derived an intense thrill from the mere act of standing talking to people while her entire body was essentially on display, clearly outlined by her clingy garment, especially since all the while she could act as though there were nothing amiss.

She had grown to enjoy watching different people's reactions, which ranged from shock, to thrill, to arousal; she had most especially delighted in surreptitiously observing the men and women whose eyes were fixated on her rear when she had her back to them and on one or two occasions she had deliberately "forgotten" her lab coat in her office when she had wanted a little extra fun.

For people she found appealing she had sometimes added a little show, such as finding a reason to bend over at the waist with her legs slightly spread, knowing that they were etching the sight into their brains. And once, in one of the small aft lifts, a crewman had pressed unnecessarily close to her from behind, and in an impulsive mischievous act she had pushed herself backwards against him, knowing he could feel her firm warmth, but before he could react more fully the doors opened and she vanished into a small crush of people returning from the commissary.

But eventually the game had grown old, and she was relieved now to be able to step back into normal clothing once again. Besides, she had Alice now to relieve her sexual tension. She could use the little redhead to vent her prurient tendencies like a steam valve popping up on a pressure cooker.

"So what did you guys think of the Captain's reaction to our little undertaking," Alice asked the ceiling.

"He sure didn't seem too concerned, did he?" said Dmitri. "Once he saw there was no hull breach he almost fell over himself getting out of there. Didn't ask a single question. Didn't even want to know why we deliberately detonated a bomb on board his ship. I have to tell you, I don't think there's going to be much of an investigation."

"Or any investigation," added Alice.

"And he didn't even raise an eyebrow when we reported Manuel's disappearance. Said he's not 'our keeper'. It was all I could do to keep from punching him in the mouth when I heard that," said Alice.

"Which means," said Vedana thoughtfully, "That he's either complicit in what's been going on here, or he doesn't care, which amounts to the same thing, really."

Alice was taking Manuel's disappearance harder than the rest of them. Vedana suspected the two might have shared a romantic moment in the past, and there was an especially sad note of loss in her voice when she spoke of him.

"Which reminds me, everyone *please* remember to wear your earbuds at all times. Starting now!" said Alice with sudden intensity. "They're fully encrypted and our only means of staying in touch with each other. I don't trust the shipboard communications systems in the slightest. And I don't want to lose anyone else – not a single one of you," she added, staring straight into Vedana's eyes.

The four scientists all paused for a moment to insert the tiny communications devices into their left ears. Alice had passed them out at the beginning of the meeting. Normally they were used for planetside excursions to keep team members connected but would serve excellently as a private onboard network within the ship.

"All the more reason we move quickly with the next step in our plan," said Alice. "It was Vedana's idea, actually. It's elegant in its simplicity and I think it'll save our bacon."

She quickly outlined the specifics of the idea to the two men, trying to fill in any details that she and Vedana had skipped over the previous evening.

While Alice spoke, Vedana idly toyed with the little redhead's tumble of hair, curling it around in her fingers. It was a pleasantly intimate gesture, and filled Alice with a comforting reminder of their budding romance.

As Alice paused briefly in her description of their intended course of action she smiled broadly up at Vedana and seductively stuck her tongue out between her lips, gently nibbling at the tip with her front teeth. It was enough to send a rush of desire coursing through the tall brunette, and Vedana felt herself blushing.

"Well, do you think we should actually attempt a real experiment?" asked Claude when Alice paused speaking. "That would mean using real compound. I think I might be more comfortable with a sham experiment instead until we've gotten to the bottom of this intrigue."

"I'm not sure about that, Claude," answered Dmitri. "Judging by the success our enemy had in sabotaging the last experiment, they appear to know what they're doing. If we set up a fake experiment and they twig to it we'll be tipping our hand. We might scare them off and never find out the means they used to alter the compound. At the very least we'll be putting them on alert. Neither case would be good for us."

"I agree," said Vedana. "All or nothing, people. In for a penny, in for a pound."

Reluctantly, Claude and Alice agreed, and plans were made to set up Lab 2 later in the afternoon in preparation for a full-blown Second Indoor Trial the following morning. Dmitri said he could fabricate some UV dust by three o'clock, so they all agreed to return at that time and set their plan in motion.

"Now if you guys don't mind," said Alice innocently, "Vedana and I have some important matters to discuss with each other… in my quarters." And both women giggled greedily.

As they watched the women leave the office, still cackling giddily, Claude turned to Dmitri and said, "I hope that's not going to become a problem."

Dmitri, who had seen Alice pass through seemingly countless relationships with both men and women over the years, said, "I don't think so, Claude. I've seen Alice with lots of lovers, but I've never her seen her look at anyone the way she looks at Vedana. I think we're going to be OK, here. Especially…" he continued after a slight pause, "If they keep passing out naked in the labs."

CHAPTER XXIII

SIGURD PACED FRANTICALLY back and forth in his little surveillance closet.

It was as bad as he had feared! Not only had the damned scientists found a way to neutralize the runaway experiment in Lab 3, but they had somehow engineered a corrective reboot in the environmental systems as well.

He was, essentially, right back at Square One. No, even worse than that, because now they would be doubly cautious and on the alert for any tiny hint that something was amiss. Even more distressing, he no longer had access to the security cameras in their offices or conference rooms. He would be hard-pressed to inflict any significant damage on their research. If things went especially well – or badly, depending on your point of view – they might have final assessments within the month and be back on Earth within 90 days.

He racked his brain searching for an avenue of attack that was still available to him but he was drawing a complete blank. Those damned nerds had covered all the bases.

He slumped down into his chair and gazed morosely at the monitor. Various messages, status reports, systems updates and the like slowly scrolled up the screen in an endless parade of ship's business.

But one particular message caught his eye as it slowly crawled up the display. He tapped a key and froze the screen and read it carefully.

It was from Boisset to the Captain, a courtesy notification that the science team would be initiating another Controlled Conditions Test the following morning in Lab 2.

He almost danced in place when he read the message.

Those idiots! Had they really learned nothing in the past week? They were going to reproduce the same event that had almost killed everyone on board the first time they tried it – with his discreet "adjustment", of course.

Sigurd saw no reason why he couldn't do again exactly what he had done the first time, only now he wouldn't wait so long before contaminating the entire science section as well.

He rubbed his hands together in glee, and sat down to run through in his mind the steps he would need to take tonight.

CHAPTER XXIV

VEDANA LAY ON her back, staring straight up into the darkness in her bedroom. Her little redhead lover snuffled gently in her sleep beside her, a tangled mound of soft curls spilling off her pillow and onto Vedana's shoulder.

But while Alice apparently had no trouble sleeping soundly – *I think I finally wore her out!* thought Vedana gleefully – Vedana's mind was racing a mile a minute as she repeatedly ran through the details of their operation, checking and rechecking and then rechecking again every step, every point, every place where they might have overlooked anything which would spoil their chances of defeating their mysterious enemy.

She was starting to relax slightly, having concluded that there was nothing they had missed, when she suddenly sat bolt upright in the bed as she thought of one horrible, catastrophic detail!

After they had prepared their booby trap this afternoon and liberally coated the lab with invisible UV dust, they had quite naturally left the module looking for all the world as though it were ready to host a critical experiment the following morning, which included, of course, locking the lab door. To leave it unlocked would have been too suspicious, a clear invitation that no clever burglar would fail to notice.

But to her horror Vedana remembered that the previous night she and Alice had taken refuge from the heat within Lab 2, and in a misguided attempt at ensuring their privacy, they had quickly reprogrammed the door lock. It was why Claude and Dmitri had been reduced to tapping helplessly on the lab's glass wall.

When you reprogrammed the door lock from inside the room, the master codes and security overrides were useless.

It was a security feature that was used to enable scientists conducting highly dangerous experiments to prevent accidental intrusion by unsuspecting visitors. The default time delay, which Vedana hadn't bothered to change, was 12 hours after entering any master code before the door would unlock, which in the event of a catastrophe would enforce a cautious assessment of the lab before breaking the seal and removing any dead bodies.

And when they had locked up the lab this evening, in her fatigue Vedana had instinctively entered the new door code, which was known to only her and Alice. Which meant that the saboteur would be unable to access the lab, and their carefully planned ambush would fail!

Vedana jumped out of bed and snatched up her bodysuit from the floor. It was the easiest and quickest garment she could put on, and in no more than a couple of seconds she had pulled it up and run barefoot out of her room and turned down the unlit corridor toward the lab.

Thank the moon and the stars she and Alice had moved to her room tonight, having exhausted the contents of Alice's fridge; besides, Vedana hadn't wanted to have to get dressed in the morning in her high heels and stockings. Alice had grabbed a change of clothes and they'd happily settled in to Vedana's cozy suite for the night.

She jogged down the darkened corridor and up to the lab door and quickly punched in her code. There was a distinctive little *click!* as the locking mechanism released, and then softly the door hissed free as the seals gave way. Vedana slipped inside and shut the door then turned to the keypad.

She paused for a moment. What code was she going to replace it with…. Then her eyes fell on a bulletin board on the opposite wall. There was just enough illumination in the room bleeding from the various machines, panels and assorted LEDs that she could make out, among the little notes, memos, cartoons and various other detritus, a scrap of paper with a series of numbers scribbled on it. It was the previous master code.

She rolled her eyes. Typical scientist behaviour. What's the best way to keep from forgetting your password? Write it down, then post the note where only you might think to look for it. The board could be seen from outside the lab, but only the person who wrote the note would think to look at it for the door access code.

Vedana quickly entered the new/old code into the keypad and was gratified to see a little green light blink in confirmation of the door's acceptance of the changed passcode. She had her hand on the door handle to let herself out when she noticed through the glass wall the slightest glimmer of light coming from the far end of the darkened corridor outside.

She froze.

The light grew fractionally brighter.

Vedana started to panic.

The light grew brighter.

Vedana spun and scanned the room. There was *literally* no place to hide! The steel tables had open shelves beneath them and there were no tall closets. Waist-high counters ran along three sides of the room, and the fourth side was a floor-to-ceiling glass wall that she could personally attest offered zero opportunity for concealment.

The light grew brighter.

Vedana briefly contemplated crouching down in the back corner of the lab but the dazzlingly-white fabric of her bodysuit rendered her almost fluorescent in the darkness. She could strip it off and hope her dark complexion might conceal her presence somewhat but she realised it would never work. She'd just end up dead *and* naked. Better to die with a shred of dignity.

The light grew brighter.

Her eyes fell on one of the waist-high cabinets beneath the counters that circled the room. Most of them were locked shut, she knew from experience, and she had no keys with her to unlock any of them. But – irrationally – one of the cabinet doors was unlocked and slightly ajar. It was the cabinet marked with an angry red diamond-shaped sticker that prominently featured a large scary flame. The cabinet where they stored the most volatile chemicals. The same ones they had used to incinerate Lab 3.

At this point the cabinet could have been filled with hissing vipers and scorpions, for all Vedana cared. She raced over to it and yanked the door open. The reason it was unlocked was immediately clear: it was all but emptied, except for one slim tubular canister of… she quickly scanned the label… PETN. The canister, which was clipped securely to a bracket inside the cabinet, was pure black and covered in urgent-looking warning labels and red stickers.

Not important. The light was really bright now. Whoever was coming was almost at the lab door.

Vedana pulled the tube of PETN off its bracket and then, folding herself up with a tiny grunt, skootched in to the cabinet sideways, on her butt, drawing her knees up to her face, tucking her head forward and pressing the soles of her feet against the opposite end of the cubbyhole. For the first time in her life she wished she were about five inches shorter. There was just barely enough room to tuck the canister of PETN under her calves and to pull the cabinet door shut.

And not a moment too soon. She could hear the keypad beeping quietly as someone entered the door access code sequence. A metallic *click!*, a pause, a hiss, and she heard a footstep inside the room.

Vedana would have bet money that her breathing could be heard throughout the whole ship, it seemed so loud to her. She opened her mouth wide and tried to calm her racing heartbeat, which was humming along at around 200 beats per minute right now.

She heard the footsteps moving quietly about the room, but they weren't wandering around aimlessly. Whoever they belonged to knew where to go and what to do. There was a quiet efficiency at work here. She heard a few little clinks, a quiet hum of some unknown machine, and the ripple of a zipper being opened and then, a second later, closed.

And then… silence.

Vedana froze. Had she done something to give herself away or left some tiny sign of her presence here?

The intruder seemed to be standing stock still in the dark lab. Listening? Examining the room? What was he doing? Vedana wanted to scream, the tension was so extreme.

And then she heard a quiet footstep come closer to her.

Then another.

The footsteps stopped directly in front of Vedana's cabinet.

She gritted her teeth, and waited for the inevitable yanking open of the cabinet door.

Should she attack first? Maybe she could surprise the intruder and club them with her canister of PETN. Then she shuddered. After what she'd seen this morning, no way was she going to be flinging around *anything* she found in this lab. Better to be shot or knifed than to be burned alive.

The seconds ticked away interminably.

And then, just when she thought she would explode like a popcorn kernel on a hot stove, she heard the footsteps suddenly turn away and move rapidly across the room.

More beeps, more clicks, a hiss, the sound of a door opening and then closing, and then silence.

She hadn't realised it, but she had been holding her breath. She didn't know how long she had been sitting there without breathing, but when the door sighed shut behind the departing intruder she released her lungs in an explosive gasp that almost made her collapse.

Pushing open the cabinet door, she tumbled out sideways and lay crumpled up on the floor, still clutching her canister of PETN. She hadn't been inside long enough for her legs to cramp up, but it still took a few seconds before she was able to pull herself upright.

Her body may have been slow to recover, but Vedana's mind was already racing. She was changing the plan. This was too good an opportunity to pass up.

But first, she needed to rouse the cavalry.

Pressing her fingertip to her earbud she whispered loudly, "Alice! ALICE! Alice wake up!" She looked around at Lab 2. Talk about déjà vu. The only difference was she couldn't shake the other woman as she had this morning.

She hoped Alice's earbud hadn't fallen out while she slept. But within seconds the response came loud and clear in her ear.

"Gaaa, mm, Vedana… is that you, hon? What's up, babe?"

"Alice, I'm in Lab 2. The enemy has just left! I was in here with them!"

The change in Alice's voice was almost a tangible thing. You could *hear* the alertness that snapped into her brain.

"You – I'm sorry, did you say you were *in the Lab with them?*"

"Ya, no time to explain. But they just left and I'm going to follow them."

"NO!" The shout almost poked a hole in Vedana's eardrum. "Vedana, you stay there! I'm coming right now. Don't you leave that lab under *any* condition, do you hear me?"

"Sorry sweetie, it's a done deal. I'm already halfway down the corridor after them."

"Vedana, I'm begging you, don't do this. You'll *die*. They'll *kill* you." The urgency in Alice's voice was extreme, but Vedana couldn't be dissuaded.

"Listen, Alice, we may never get another chance like this. We don't know for sure that the UV powder will work. And they might even have stolen some of the compound. I'm pretty sure I heard what sounded like the clink of a test tube. I need to ID this person right now. I promise I'll stay out of sight." *If I can,* she added silently.

Alice knew when she was beat, but she wasn't going to just lay down for this.

"Give me reports if you can," she said. "Tell me where you're going. I'll try to catch up and join you."

"Roger, babe," whispered Vedana. "Right now we're midships on the, um, the starboard side, and I'm heading up a metal stairwell of some kind that I think leads to an exit portal on… um, I can't tell. I think it's some kind of tower."

"OK, I'm right behind you. I'll be there in a minute, hon."

CHAPTER XXV

CAPTAIN VAN DEEP leaned over the railing and inhaled a long, deep lungful of the icy cold air.

He enjoyed coming up here late at night when the ship was asleep to look at the stars and gather his thoughts. He cradled in his right fist his hand-carved Meerschaum pipe filled with the aromatic tobacco blend he was addicted to.

Tobacco was illegal, of course, but if anyone had access to contraband, starship Captains were the ones. The pipe was a silly affectation, a relic from centuries long past, but it pleased him to no end to hold it and imagine himself some intrepid adventurer at the helm of a 17th century whaler, bounding through the waves in pursuit of his own white whale. He took a long, deliberate pull on his pipe and then watched the smoke billow out of his lips before rapidly vanishing into the night as the swirling wind whipped it away.

This batch of tobacco was especially choice, and he had been saving it for a special occasion. Since tonight was the last night of his life, he figured it was pretty special.

He looked up at the night sky. A storm was coming in, he mused. He shivered slightly against the chilly wind rapidly increasing in intensity as the first tentative spits of slushy rain pattered randomly across the ice-covered deck. He considered for a moment then concluded he still had a few minutes left to enjoy the night before conditions deteriorated too much. He took another pull on his pipe.

The day's developments had been pleasing and distressing all at once.

He certainly couldn't complain about the complete restoration of the life support program and the blessed relief of once again being able to sit on the Bridge without soaking his uniform with sweat.

Less pleasant was the realization that the scientists on board had somehow once again firmly wrested control of their dangerous science experiment from whoever had been obstructing them. The final nail in the coffin had been the memo that they intended to recommence their research.

He was certain they would be successful. Despite disliking them personally, he begrudgingly respected their intellects and their devotion to their trade. He had no doubt they would eventually succeed in their endeavour.

Which left him little choice, of course.

They couldn't be allowed to complete the project and to transmit their final data back to Earth. Before that happened, they must be stopped.

In light of today's events, he sadly concluded that there was only one way to do this.

And so he had decided that tomorrow morning he would get up, shave, shower, put on his full dress uniform, and go down to engineering and overload the fusion reactor. The ship and all its horrible poison would be obliterated in one magnificent, spectacular explosion.

He was standing there, leaning on the rail contemplating this imminent conclusion to their journey, when suddenly a figure – a woman, he thought – clothed head to toe in a white bodysuit burst into view, evidently just as surprised to find him here as he was to find her, as she froze motionless when she caught sight of him.

She was about 30 meters distant, at the top of a tall wide conning tower that reared up over him toward midships. The tower was another affectation, a useless addition to the ship's superstructure that her original designers had added in their attempts to make a starship resemble an ocean liner.

Against the darkness of the night, through the sleet which was now pelting down from the sky, he could just barely make out her white-clad form, but couldn't see her face – or even her head at all, really; it seemed as though her body stopped at her shoulders. It was an eerie sight and unnerved him. The howl of the storm, rapidly increasing with a real vengeance, whipped away his voice as he called out to her.

"You there! What are you doing up there? Come down from there this instant! That's very dangerous!" and he gesticulated with his right hand for her to come down, pointing at her and the conning tower.

She did something with her arm that he couldn't quite make out and he squinted through the night, trying to get a clearer view.

CHAPTER XXVI

VEDANA CLIMBED the stairs as rapidly – and as stealthily – as she could.

Wouldn't do to meet anyone coming down while I'm on my way up, she reflected.

"Where are you now?" came the voice in her ear.

"Still climbing," she whispered. "I think they might be too far ahead, though. I don't see the light any more. I'm going as fast as I can but I don't want to accidentally rush into anyone who might be waiting in the dark."

Alice all but moaned in agony. "Oh, Vedana, pleeeeeease don't get yourself killed. Can't you hang back a bit and wait for me?"

"Hold on," whispered Vedana, "I'm at the top. There's a pressure door here. I'm going to take a look."

For Alice the silence was excruciating while she waited for Vedana to respond. She didn't want to prompt her for any more information lest she cause her to speak and give herself away to the enemy.

"OK, I'm outside. It's an observation tower or something. I can see markings on the bulkheads below me. Looks like I'm about 10 meters or so above Deck 9. Damn, there's some kind of really nasty storm going on. The wind is vicious. There's no one he– wait. There's a man. He sees me. God, I can't tell, but I think it's the Captain. I can't see for shit through this storm. It's really dark out here."

"Vedana get out of there *now,*" shrieked Alice.

"Oh my God," said Vedana. "He has a gun or something. He's pointing it at me. Oh my God."

The next Alice heard was an explosion so massive that she was knocked off her feet, her earbud cut out and the sound went dead.

CHAPTER XXVII

VEDANA HADN'T realised it but she'd completely lost Sigurd's trail as he took his usual exit onto Deck 9 and trotted toward his hiding place behind the maintenance panel.

So while he crept surreptitiously in the darkness along Deck 9, she continued to climb up to the top of a conning tower about 10 meters above him.

When she came out into the night the chill of the air and the blast of the wind almost knocked her backward. The insanely thin fabric of her bodysuit was more insulative than one would have guessed, but it still wasn't enough to block the sting from the icicles of sleet that assaulted her. Her bare feet burned in pain at the icy bite of the frigid platform. The subzero gale buffeted her and whipped her hair around her head as she staggered over to the rail at the edge of the platform.

When she saw the Captain she started to panic. Alice was shrieking in her ear and the menacing form on the deck below her was yelling incomprehensibly and pointing some kind of hand weapon at her and her animal instincts just took over and she reared back and flung the dark black canister she was still gripping in her hand.

She felt time stand still as she watched the canister first sail up through the air and then disappear into the inky blackness of the night as it followed its arc down to the man below her on the deck.

She really didn't know what would happen when the canister hit the deck. She was hoping that, at the very least, it would startle him sufficiently to allow her to duck back into the tower and make her escape.

The tremendous explosion that blossomed out from the spot where the canister impacted the deck knocked her unconscious and threw her back at least twenty feet, to land insensate on the far side of the icy cold platform at the top of the tower.

The Captain's body was instantly vapourised along with any indication that he had ever been there. The railing was completely torn off the edge of the deck and flung several hundred meters away from the ship. Amazingly, the decking retained its integrity, and although it was buckled and caved-in right at the point of impact, most of the blast had been reflected up and away from the ship. A few pieces of equipment and some random small structures on the deck had been swept clear away, but for the most part the damage was fairly limited.

Sigurd, who was at the far end of the ship, was knocked off his feet by the explosion. As was anyone else inside the ship who happened to be standing up at the time. Claude and Dmitri were both knocked out of their bunks, along with the rest of the sleeping crew, and Alice was flung against a bulkhead as she raced along an internal corridor on Deck 8.

Sigurd looked at the enormous fireball rising up from the forward end of the ship and said, "What the hell is going on now?"

He decided this was too important not to investigate immediately. Turning away from his path toward his hiding spot he jogged rapidly back up the deck in the direction he had come, grimly tucking his chin down to help shield his eyes from the freezing rain.

Vedana regained consciousness fairly quickly, thanks mostly to the frigid sleet that peppered her face. She opened and closed her jaw and tried to pop her ears; she didn't think she had blown out her eardrums. *Thank goodness for small mercies.* She put a hand to her head, then felt around on her body for broken bones, and then groggily staggered to her feet.

Well.

That was a surprise.

Guess it's good I didn't hit that intruder with that canister in the lab. She shuddered to think how close she'd come to obliterating herself. *Boy, would Alice have been pissed!*

She reached up to tap the earbud in her left ear but it wasn't there, and she realised she must have lost it in the explosion.

Carefully and deliberately, her vision spinning like a mad carousel, she stumbled over to the access door and firmly gripped the stair railing as she slowly began the descent from the tower platform, focusing intently on the metal lattice of each stair as she painstakingly placed each foot on the next step down. When she had descended about halfway down the staircase from where she'd entered off Deck 8 she noticed an access door off to the side of a small landing with a sign marked "Deck 9", a door that she'd completely missed in the darkness during her initial pursuit.

That explains why I couldn't find my guy, she thought.

A strange feeling nagging in a corner of her mind made her pause. Her head was clearing and she was feeling better, and it occurred to her that maybe she should go out onto the deck and take a look around. As long as she was here anyway.

She gritted her teeth at the thought of facing that cold again, and looked down sympathetically at her poor frozen toes, but put the thought out of her mind and pulled the door open and stepped out onto the deck.

And came face to face with Sigurd on his way toward the blast site.

CHAPTER XXVIII

$\mathbf{A}$LICE WAS RACING along the interior corridor on Deck 8. She had used up precious seconds getting dressed before she left Vedana's room; thank goodness she had brought along a pair of stirrup pants and sneakers to wear tomorrow. Unfortunately, she had only a lightweight t-shirt but that couldn't be helped now.

She rubbed her left elbow. The explosion that had rocked the ship a moment back had thrown her like a rag doll against the bulkhead, and she counted herself lucky not to have broken anything. She refused to allow herself to contemplate what it might have done to Vedana.

Anxious as she was to get to Vedana, she forced herself to detour to the nearest equipment room on her path. She didn't know if Vedana was alive or dead, and her earbud had gone out. She might have only one way to locate her, and she needed to grab it now.

She got to the room she was looking for and impatiently keyed in her access code. When the latch released she all but kicked the door open in her rush to get to the stores inside.

Immediately she spotted it. "UV" was the only marking on its side, but that made it clear enough that this torch shone a UV beam, much as a normal flashlight shines visible light.

She clicked it on but of course couldn't see any difference. *I hope to hell it doesn't need new batteries or something,* she thought as she spun around and raced out of the room toward the nearest outside access door.

The closest stairwell Alice could locate was excruciatingly far down the ship. She felt she had run almost all the way to the stern before she finally spotted it. She virtually leapt up the stairs and threw herself at the exit door at the top. She spun the wheel and yanked the door open and leapt outside, flicking the light on and pointing it down at the deck.

She was immediately rewarded with two distinct sets of footprints, although she noted with concern that the storm was rapidly eradicating most of the markings. Already she couldn't make out clearly what kind of feet had made the tracks, nor even in which direction they were traveling. The wind and sleet from the storm pierced her t-shirt as though it weren't even there and within seconds she was soaked, but such was her panic that she barely even noticed.

A mental flip of the coin and she turned to her right and continued running toward the stern, reasoning that if there were tracks here, they must be leading in that direction, since the people who had made the tracks had almost certainly come from farther forward on the ship.

It was a fine theory but didn't console her in the least when she came to the place where the tracks abruptly stopped, along with a smear of UV powder, and then reversed course. Cursing bitterly under her breath, she turned and ran at her top speed back up the deck toward the bow of the ship.

CHAPTER XXIX

VEDANA WAS just as startled as Sigurd when he all but ran right into her, but he hadn't expected to find anyone else up here, while she was on guard for exactly that eventuality. It worked in her favour.

"HO!" she grunted, as she rammed both her outstretched arms straight into his chest, knocking him backward and off his feet.

Before he could gather himself up she had already spun around and was now racing up the deck like an Olympic sprinter.

Sigurd took off up the deck after her, but he was already winded from his jog up from the stern and was visibly flagging as their chase lengthened. But he was dressed for the outside while Vedana was having trouble just staying on her feet on the ice-covered deck. Her bare toes slid treacherously with each long bound of her legs, and she couldn't maintain sufficient grip on the surface to pick up any appreciable speed.

A small snow bank blocked her path and she leapt over it, but she slipped a bit on takeoff and one of her feet failed to clear it. She tumbled onto the deck, smashing her face down onto a jagged sheet of sharp ice crystals.

Groggily she stood up again and briefly glanced down at the obstacle that had tripped her up. Half-covered with ice, Manuel's frozen form stretched out before her, one hand desperately reaching out and above his head, as though he were trying to swim to safety.

She stood there, stifling a scream of horror and fear as a cascade of blood dripped down from the gashes torn into her face and forehead by the spiky pile of ice crystals she had fallen into.

Huffing and puffing, Sigurd caught up to her at that moment. He paused briefly, and the two of them stood there in the howling wind and freezing rain, panting heavily, hands on their knees, each warily eyeing the other, Manuel's frozen form laying between them. They looked for all the world like a pair of very skinny Sumo wrestlers angling for the best position.

Sigurd slowly and deliberately reached down into his side pocket and withdrew a long screwdriver. A knife would have been much better, he thought, but he'd had no reason to believe he would need such a thing. Still, this would do just as well. His screwdriver was perfectly designed to pierce that flimsy fabric and rip a hole in her aorta. He knew exactly where to thrust it. *One jab'll do the job*, he reflected, and prepared to leap over Manuel and deliver the killing blow.

Sigurd was just about to make his move when he seemed to explode up and out of the snow as he rocketed past Vedana to crash face-first against the railing behind her.

Alice had seen them from about 15 meters away and had used the intervening distance to increase her speed as much as she possibly could before leaping into the air and ramming both her knees into Sigurd's back.

Normally such a blow might even have broken his spine, but Sigurd had worn a heavy coat in preparation for tonight's excursion, and the combination of the coat's padding and its icy slick exterior had diminished the effect of Alice's attack. Her knees skidded off him without making a solid impact and all she succeeded in doing was to knock the breath out of him as he tumbled forward into the railing.

Alice meanwhile bounced off to the side and crumpled up into the snow. She hadn't landed well and Vedana frantically rushed over to her prone form and turned her over. Alice's eyes were closed and Vedana slapped her face and called her name. Slowly, Alice's eyelids fluttered a bit and she opened her eyes.

Just at that moment Vedana felt herself torn up and off Alice by Sigurd, who spun her around and gripped her neck tightly in both his ice cold hands. His screwdriver had flown free of his grasp when Alice had struck him but he didn't need any tool to wring the life out of these two women and he proceeded to clench ever more tightly the struggling woman's throat as she flailed around desperately beneath his crushing grip.

Maybe it was a tickling sensation in his chest, or maybe it was the look he spotted in Vedana's eyes as she stared in horror at a spot below his chin, but something made Sigurd pause briefly and glance down at his jacket.

A magnificent blossom of iridescent white crystal needles was rapidly spreading up and out from his jacket's zippered breast pocket, where the shattered tip of a broken test tube protruded from the fabric.

When Alice had sent Sigurd reeling into the iron railing he had impacted with his chest not just hard enough to knock the wind out of him but also hard enough to shatter the delicate vial of death that he carried around in his pocket.

As Sigurd realised what had just happened he momentarily relaxed his grip on Vedana's neck but suddenly his eyes snapped into focus and with venomous malevolence he quickly slipped his hands down and gripped her by her upper arms.

Glaring viciously into her eyes, as the cold slowly began to clench his heart and lungs in its icy embrace, he said, "Fuck… You… *Bitch!*"

And with his last ounce of strength he pulled Vedana violently against his chest and stabbed the jagged end of the dripping test tube into her.

Vedana recoiled in horror and she fell backward onto the ice, Sigurd's now-frozen fingers locked on her arms with his body coming to rest pressing down on top of her.

Vedana shrieked in terror and frantically tried to yank her arms out of Sigurd's frozen grasp but she couldn't tear free. She could almost feel the freezing compound dripping down and spreading through her bodysuit as it invaded her body to freeze her solid.

Alice came to the rescue, quickly staggering to her feet and then stomping down on Sigurd's hands, first one and then the other, which shattered into a million tiny fragments under her shoe. Vedana pushed Sigurd up and off her as forcefully as she could and he tumbled off to the side, his face frozen in an evil rictus of rage.

Still laying supine on her back, she raised her head to look down at herself, expecting to see a nightmare spiderweb of frosty tendrils spreading across her chest but she saw nothing except a few wet drops of silvery liquid sitting puddled up on her sternum like bubbles of oil floating in a saucer of water.

"Oh my God, Vedana, don't fucking move an inch," hissed Alice and she quickly moved around to kneel above the terrified woman's head as she lay trembling on the ice.

Carefully, Alice reached down and grasped both of Vedana's wrists then quickly pulled her arms up and back until they were reaching straight up from Vedana's head. Then, gripping the recumbent woman by her shoulders, she forcefully and quickly twisted her over onto her face, then rolled her again and again, rolling her like a white fleshy log across the deck until she was sure there was no compound left clinging to her bodysuit.

"Come on," said Alice urgently. "We've gotta run before it can spread across the deck and get on us!"

And both women jumped to their feet and took off running down the deck toward the nearest access hatch, which they slammed and locked into place behind them before collapsing. Panting, shivering, sweating and bleeding, but wonderfully, gloriously, exuberantly, ALIVE.

CHAPTER XXX

ALICE SAT HUNCHED over Vedana, deftly dabbing at her face with a cotton ball. Vedana lay back in the chair yelping occasionally but mostly putting up with the other woman's ministrations.

In the days that had passed since Vedana's encounter with Sigurd her three fellow scientists had been busy tying up loose ends while she lay in her quarters letting her wounds and her frozen toes heal and recovering from the concussion she had suffered during the explosion.

They'd retrieved Manuel's and Sigurd's frozen corpses and brought them inside. Manuel was currently stored in the ship's morgue where he could remain until his body was delivered to his family on his homeworld. Alice was especially happy that they could afford him that last small dignity.

Sigurd's corpse was also stored in the morgue, but the only reason they didn't incinerate it and eject the ashes onto the planet was they needed to keep him as evidence. Global Dynamics would be pleased not to have to pay any death benefits to Sigurd's family – even for one of the largest corporations in the galaxy, a dollar is still a dollar, after all.

Vedana yelped as Alice brushed a spot that was still a little tender.

"Oh don't be such a baby," Alice scolded playfully. "Take it like a man."

Dmitri barked out a laugh from where he sat behind Claude's desk. "Now *there's* a phrase I never thought I'd hear from you two," he chuckled.

Alice shot him the evil eye and he quickly wiped the smile from his face, feigning contrition.

Claude entered the room and smiled broadly at Vedana. "Nice to see you up and about, my dear. The team wasn't the same without you."

"Sounds to me like you've been doing just fine," retorted Vedana, as Alice straightened up and put away her ointments.

"Well, it's true we were able to get a better view of the whole picture, but I think everyone will enjoy hearing Dmitri's report this morning – I believe he's figured out the final piece of the puzzle."

All eyes turned to Dmitri, who cleared his throat and took a deep breath.

"OK, now that Claude's here let's get right to it. We'll take it from the top.

"We know from what Vedana's told us that someone entered Lab 2 and stole a vial of the compound, as well as tampering with the supply that he left behind.

"Now, at first Vedana assumed that our intruder was the Captain, as he was the first person she spotted outside on Deck 9 and she was never able to get a look at the person while she hid in the lab. But I think we can all agree that the real intruder was actually this Sigurd person, the one who attacked her later."

"But we were still left with several questions, such as: why was the Captain outside and what did he have to do with this whole set of events, and what did Sigurd do in the lab module and how was he able to alter our compound?"

"He spent a long time in there," said Vedana. "At least, it seemed to me that he did. I heard him doing a bunch of things and then he was quiet for one or two minutes, and then he suddenly left."

"So you told us, as I recall," said Dmitri. "But I think I've reconstructed his activity there to account for all his actions, second by second."

He had their attention now, and they all listened carefully in rapt silence.

"As soon as Sigurd entered the room he immediately went to the refrigerated cabinet where the solution was stored and set about changing its molecular structure, using the same method as before. He evidently thought that if we had two failed experiments in a row we would conclude the original formula was faulty and that we'd either give up or at the very least go back to the drawing board. Maybe he planned to kill us off one by one while we continued to work at finding a solution."

A collective shudder passed through the group as they listened to Dmitri's casual reference to their possible deaths. As scientists they had little affinity for violence and were appalled to consider that someone might have been planning to murder them all merely to stop their research.

"Possibly as a backup plan, or maybe to keep some of the compound to sell to another party, he then took a small amount and saved it in a test tube, which he then apparently dropped into a zippered breast pocket in his jacket. He then left the room, whereupon Vedana chased after him."

"Wait," said Vedana. "You skipped a part. I told you I heard him doing those things, but then he came over to where I was hiding and did nothing for about a minute before he left. What do you think was happening there?"

Dmitri actually reddened a tiny bit and cleared his throat and said, "Ah. Yes. Well, he wasn't actually doing 'nothing'. I think I have an idea what might have caught his attention for a moment."

Dmitri reached down into a small drawer in Claude's desk and extracted a little flat slab of black glass, about the size of a pack of playing cards. He put it on the table and held his hand near it, but didn't touch it.

"As you might recognise, this is a simple holo projector. Most of us have one in our quarters or on our desk with pictures of our friends and family back home, but usually the device just sits and projects our photos automatically, repeatedly cycling through the stored set of images.

"This one though, I'm pretty certain was Manuel's; he spent a lot of time working in Lab 2. Well, Manuel apparently changed the settings on this device from 'auto display' to 'display on touch only'. You just touch it with your fingers anywhere on the device to activate the projection."

He briefly touched the slab and a little image popped into view, hovering just above the projector, and then vanished as Dmitri removed his fingers.

"I think Sigurd might have spotted it. Perhaps he noticed Manuel looking at it one day while he surveilled him in the lab.

"This was sitting on the counter directly above the cabinet where you were hiding, Vedana. While you were cowering in terror, Sigurd was actually standing there looking at these pictures." And once again Dmitri touched his fingers to the slab of glass and again a little image popped into view.

The image showed an attractive, scantily-clad young woman looking at the camera with a seductive expression. After a few seconds it switched to another image of a different woman in a similar pose, and a few seconds after that, another one.

"It appears that Manuel kept a little archive of… ah, his previous… shall we say, 'conquests', and enjoyed looking through it from time to time when he was at work."

Alice, her face suddenly beet red, reached out and snatched the glass slab off the desk and thrust it into her pocket.

"I think we owe Manuel some privacy," she said quickly. "There's no need to see those pictures."

The two men tried – unsuccessfully – to hide their amusement, but doing his best to keep a straight face Dmitri just said, "Right. Absolutely."

Vedana grinned and thought to herself that she absolutely needed to get her hands on that slab of glass. There was probably one photo in there that she just *had* to see.

"So let me get this straight," said Vedana. "This guy breaks into our lab in the middle of the night in a life-and-death operation of extreme importance, and he stops to look at dirty pictures?"

"What can I say," replied Dmitri, shrugging his shoulders and spreading his hands wide. *"Men."*

Everyone nodded quietly. *And the worst part,* reflected Vedana silently, *is that no one is surprised in the least.*

"But moving on…" continued Dmitri, "Vedana, you chased Sigurd but missed the exit door he'd gone through and instead you climbed the stairs to the top of the conning tower. Then you went out onto the observation platform, where you spotted Captain van Deep."

"Right. And he pointed a small hand weapon at me. What was it, exactly? Did you get a chance to recover it?"

"Sadly, Vedana, the explosion which took our dear Captain's life also effectively wiped him from existence. It disintegrated him so completely that not even a trace of his DNA remains. I took a medical scanner up onto the deck to try to confirm his identity, but unfortunately he was absolutely obliterated in the blast. The crew has no idea what happened to him and are assuming that Sigurd disposed of him somehow. I saw no good reason to disabuse them of this suspicion. When they asked about the explosion I feigned ignorance.

"Which reminds me, Vedana, I never heard from you what it actually was that you threw at him. Can you remember what that substance was?"

"I remember perfectly. It was labeled 'PETN'."

Manuel looked up sharply from a note he had been scribbling. He put his pen down slowly and said, carefully and clearly, "Wait. Are you sure about that? It said 'P-E-T-N'?"

"Yes, of course I'm sure," replied Vedana impatiently. "It was a little black tube of some kind covered with red warning stickers and clearly marked, 'PETN'."

"And let me get this straight, you ran through the ship carrying this tube?"

"Yessss…" answered Vedana.

"And you climbed a set of stairs and then ran over a slippery deck in the middle of a storm still carrying it?"

Vedana was getting exasperated, but she noticed how pale Dmitri's face had become.

"Yes, I already told you I did. It didn't get up there by itself, you know."

"No, of course not, Vedana, but just let me tell you that this 'little tube', as you so blithely refer to it, is actually called a 'Shock-tube', a self-activated electronic shock-type detonator used in heavy demolition and containing an explosive whose full scientific name is Pentaerythritol Tetranitrate, which is approximately 1,000 times more explosive than nitroglycerin.

"And it's so unstable that the only safe way to transport PETN *– or even to carry it from room to room,*" he added with emphasis "*–* is in a motion-stabilized transport container."

He put his head in his hands.

"And you ran through the ship swinging it around like you were on a running track with a five-pound weight in your hand."

Alice, who had been standing, sat down hard. Her face was white as a sheet.

Vedana knew how she felt. She was dizzy too, even though she was sitting down.

"Well, all I can say, young lady, is that some very special group of gods must be looking out for you. If I ever buy a lottery ticket, I want you to pick it out for me."

Their laughter perfectly defused the tension.

"Well, where was I… oh yes. While you were doing all this apparently our friend Sigurd was running along Deck 9 for some unknown purpose. Most likely he was going to hide the test tube of compound somewhere up there, which would explain why he was carrying a screwdriver."

A shudder passed through Vedana as she recalled the weapon, but she forced herself to focus on Dmitri's voice.

"Judging from his tracks that Alice followed, when he saw your little pyrotechnics display go up, he turned and came back up the deck to investigate. Lucky for all of us that he did so, too, because if he'd had the chance to stash it away none of us would be here right now talking about this."

"Aaaaaand, the rest you all know. Fight in the snow, the cavalry" – he glanced at Alice – "shows up in the nick of time, test tube breaks, bad guy freezes to death, happy ending."

"Oh no you don't, bub," said Vedana. "You're not getting off that easy. Why aren't I dead? That compound was all over me. I should have been a human ice cube before Alice could even get back on her feet."

"Oh, that's easy," answered Dmitri casually. "It's that suit of yours."

Here he reached over and picked up Vedana's heat suit, which had been laying on top of a box to his side.

"This material isn't just the most obscene fabric in the world –" Vedana quickly blushed – "It's also insanely resilient, durable, and almost impervious to damage.

"It's quite probable that even if Sigurd had been able to stab you with his screwdriver he wouldn't have been able to puncture your garment. True, you would have been just as wounded, because the suit would have flexed with the weapon, but its integrity would have been undamaged."

Here, to demonstrate his point, Dmitri held up the suit and poked at it forcefully with a letter opener from Claude's desk.

"Hey hey hey," shouted Vedana, "Easy there with the merchandise, fella!"

Dmitri rolled his eyes and put down the letter opener.

"When Sigurd pressed himself up against you not only was the broken test tube unable to pierce your suit, but our compound simply sat on top of the fabric without finding any organic substance to activate its freezing process. It was as though the chemical were still in its test tube – it needs an organic surface to react with to become active. Even cotton or wool will suffice. Thankfully, this suit is neither."

"Which explains why I've got a nasty welt on my chest from where the jagged tip of the test tube poked into me through my suit, but no actual freeze damage."

"Precisely."

"Why didn't the solution pass through the suit, the way my perspiration does?"

"Because the fabric's molecular structure is porous in only one direction. It vents moisture but doesn't absorb any. It's quite marvelous, actually. I think I'll get one for myself."

Judging by their expressions, everyone in the room suddenly imagined what Dmitri would look like clothed in a similar garment. Thankfully, Claude broke in and changed the subject.

"I see you've saved the best for last, Dmitri," he said meaningfully.

"Hmm? Oh, well, I had to keep their attention, didn't I?" answered Dmitri, grinning, then said, "So obviously you all have one last, final question in your minds: *What did Sigurd do to our compound to alter it?*

"The answer to that question lies in a problem first identified all the way back in the early years of the 21st century – we call it *'the hand sanitizer paradox'*.

"You may remember that back around the time of the first of the modern pandemics, people thought they could avoid getting sick by slathering their hands with alcohol-based solutions –" a little shudder passed through the group – "or by pathologically wiping down every surface in sight with a similar substance.

"And even though they knew quite well that these solutions are toxic endocrine disrupters that interfere with or even eliminate the natural hormones that regulate our bodies' development, behaviour, fertility, and normal cell metabolism, most people were too lazy to wash their hands with soap and water and instead settled for the quick fix of squirting on their hands what was essentially poison.

"Ironically, it was precisely this behaviour that was the catalyst for the emergence of the 'super bugs' that almost exterminated mankind at the end of that century. The disinfectants' manufacturers had boasted that their products killed '99.9%' of the germs. Apparently, no one ever bothered to consider what might result from the .1% of the germs that survived, and how resilient *their* offspring would be.

"You all know the rest of the story, so I won't bore you with any further ancient history, but this is in fact exactly what our homicidal saboteur did to the compound."

"He poured hand sanitizer on it?" asked Alice sarcastically.

"Well, in a sense, yes.

"When we recovered his body we found this little machine in his inside jacket pocket. It's a portable microwave emitter."

Dmitri picked up a small implement that looked uncannily like a ray gun from a vintage science fiction illustration.

"I think his original intention was to kill the compound so that our experiment would fail miserably. But he didn't quite hit it with a strong enough dose. He did succeed in killing almost all of the active compound, but a fractional amount remained, altered in a very significant way.

"Our compound, as you know, breaks down in the wild after just a few hours, but the irradiated compound has no such time limit on its cellular integrity because the chemical structure that is responsible for its degradation is modified when it's hit with a strong blast of electromagnetic radiation."

"Then we're screwed," said Alice. "We can never release it on Earth because any lunatic with a microwave oven can turn it into a planet killer."

"Not so fast, Alice," said Dmitri. "Nature is never that pure and simple.

"As mankind has painfully come to be aware, every action has it own reaction, and for once this may actually work in our favour. It's not unlike trying to synthesize painkillers from the opium poppy; the two best derivatives are morphine and heroin, which are natural substances extracted from the plant. But as soon as science tries removing the opioid effects, the painkilling benefits diminish quite significantly.

"The same principle is at work here with our compound. When the limits on the compound's natural decay are removed, one side effect is that it also becomes much more fragile and is easily damaged by the elements.

"The sample we had in the lab was being run under controlled conditions. It wasn't being exposed to wind, rain, sun, and rapid swings in temperature. So its growth continued unabated because it was occurring in such a safe, benign environment.

"And I've determined that Manuel, who apparently was attacked much the same way you were, Vedana, was exposed to the same altered solution that was in our failed lab trial. But because that compound was deployed outdoors, and subject to assault from the weather, it broke down before it could cover more than a few hundred square meters across the ship's surface. That's why the entire ship isn't encased in a giant block of ice right now.

"The altered solution will never be a huge threat to anyone outside a laboratory environment. It couldn't infect more than half an acre of land, at most, before becoming completely inert. Our project is saved."

"Hear, hear!" said Claude merrily.

"That's wonderful news, Dmitri," added Alice.

Only Vedana remained still pensive, looking a bit puzzled.

"As delighted as I am to hear that, Dmitri, I can't help but wonder: if Sigurd had that emitter on him when he attacked me, why didn't he just shoot me with it and boil my insides?"

"He might have, if he'd known you were coming. But I think you took him by surprise. These handheld versions take about five minutes to charge up," said Dmitri, blithely waving the gun around in the air before them.

"Yow! You wanna not point that sucker at me, please?" cried Alice, raising her hand up and waving it at Dmitri.

"What did I just say, Alice?"

"Yeah, I heard you. I also don't know if that thing doesn't store some kind of residual charge and I don't want my tombstone to say, 'Oops!'"

EPILOGUE

LATER THAT NIGHT, as Vedana and Alice snuggled up together, Alice raised herself up onto one elbow, looked over at Vedana and stared into her eyes.

"Well now that this project is drawing to a close, I guess we'll all be moving on."

"Mm-hmm…" replied Vedana, smiling hazily at her little firecracker of a lover.

"Do you… that is, have you given any thought to… what you'll be doing… next…?" Alice asked hesitantly, almost afraid to put the thought into words.

"Well," said Vedana, "The galaxy's a big place. There's unlimited opportunity and an endless list of places to go.

"But I'm pretty certain of one thing in particular."

"Which is…" prompted Alice.

"Which is, that no matter where I go, where I work or who I work with… I'm doing it with you."

Whereupon, squealing in exhilarated relief, Alice collapsed down against Vedana, buried her face in the crook of her neck and shoulder, and went to sleep with the biggest smile on her face that she had ever worn.

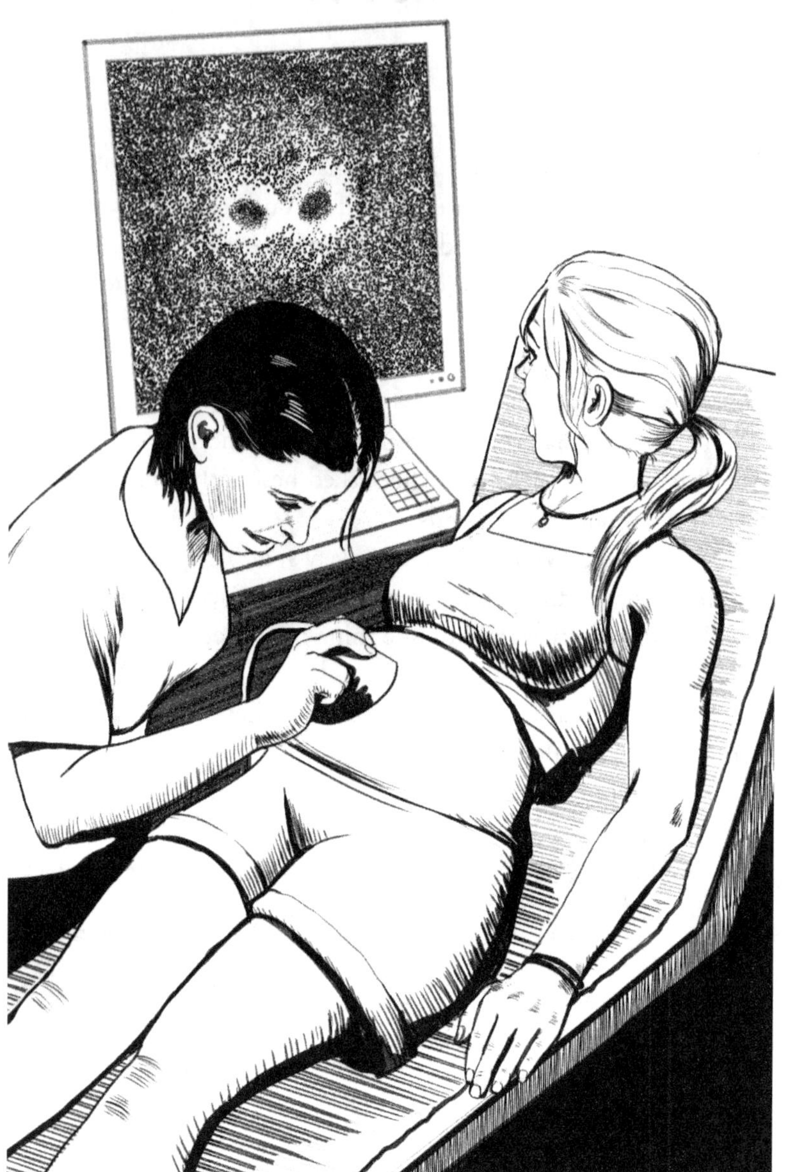

prodigy

SEPTEMBER, 1998

JILL SPRINTED as fast as she could, dodging pedestrians, bicyclists, cars, cutting across lawns and intersections. Campus was especially busy this morning. It seemed to her that every enrolled student was out — *Out to get in my way*, she grumbled as she wove a complicated pattern through the crowds.

It figured: the last sunny day probably until March and everyone and their dog was outside enjoying the fresh air. *But why do they all have to be in my way?!*

Jill had hurried across this quiet collection of buildings, quads and paths many times in the last four years. She had gotten to the point where she regarded the area as "hers", attaching significance to various places: an old maple tree where she'd nervously waited once for a first date, jacked-up on adrenaline and anticipation; a costume supply shop that had had the misfortune to be her first employer (Jill remembered virtually nothing of her work experience there – her memories all centered on the cute guy in the medieval armour section who had been the ultimate cause of her dismissal); a late-night cafe where she and her girlfriends complained about men and sympathised with each other in weekly study sessions that were anything but.

Today, however, these recollections barely pierced the periphery of her consciousness. Right now the only thought on her mind was getting across campus as quickly as possible.

How could I let myself be late! How screwed up can I be, I can't believe this!

How strange, her sleeping in like that. Dead to the world until almost nine this morning, yet she'd woken up at eight a.m. probably every morning since she was twelve years old. It was one thing she did particularly well and now when she had really depended on it – *nothing*.

She jogged around a corner past a small Victorian long since converted into an administrative office for the university; she'd never been inside and had no idea what they did there but would have been the first to show up with a protest sign if the house were threatened with demolition. Jill believed strongly in the importance of diversity in the campus structures.

She hoped her new job was in a nice old building like that, a place with real character. So far all her contact with her new employer – both her initial inquiry and the call back last night – had been by phone and she hadn't recognised the address where they'd told her to show up.

The walk signal at the next corner changed to a red hand just as she arrived and Jill took the opportunity to stop and catch her breath. She leaned against a metal box stuffed with newspapers, resting a hand on her thigh, puffing, feeling perspiration collecting under her clothes. That was puzzling. She hadn't been running that long this morning, and she was in great shape. She combed through her recent memories for an explanation – no beer last night, no partying at all for the last few months, in fact. And last night she'd even turned in early. No answer there.

Regardless, Jill decided she'd just have to stop rushing: it wouldn't do to arrive all hot and sweaty. She was already late, so she might as well look good when she did arrive. They'd told her casual was fine and she'd chosen a white shirt and bubblegum-pink sweatshirt, clean jeans and tennis shoes. Tying her strawberry blonde hair back into a ponytail was the best solution this morning since she'd woken too late to curl it. The end result was that she presented the perfect picture of sweetness and American beauty, the classic image of Miss Co-Ed U.S.A.

She wasn't sure that's what they wanted, though. In fact she knew almost nothing about what her new job entailed. The phone call she'd gotten last night had been very one-sided: a pleasant soft old-man voice floating meaningless questions down the phone line, a conversation she'd experienced more in the periphery of her mind than in her foreground consciousness.

Question: How much do you want this job? *What a strange question for a job interview,* she thought. And she hadn't known what to say because, in truth, she really *didn't* want to take this position. She couldn't fathom what in God's Name had prompted her to answer the ad she saw on the web – some unexplainable whim had momentarily overcome her, and she had promptly forgotten about it almost immediately afterward.

She already had her career on track and she loved it and she *certainly* had no intention of quitting for some dead-end lab job she'd found in the classifieds.

She'd opened her mouth to tell the voice that she'd made a mistake, that the caller was wasting his time; she didn't want the position after all.

Before she could say anything, though, the voice had told her to wait, to think about her answer, to delve deep into her mind to root out her most basic, most primal motivation, to consider carefully and not to speak out loud, not until the voice told her to. And then another question and another, all suffixed by the bizarre instruction not to speak the answers. Question: Why do you think you can do this? *Do what?* she'd wanted to scream, *I don't know what you do!* The ad had provided no more information than a phone number and "graduate student wanted for lab work". A description that vague could entail anything, from decapitating mice in the insulin lab to entering statistics into a computer.

She'd wanted to end the call but the voice was compelling; she did as it told her: she thought and kept quiet.

Then the tenor of the call changed and she found herself drawn into a relaxed conversation with the voice about nothing at all: the weather, college, life in general; she couldn't remember anything specific but when it was over she had a new job and an address and a time to start.

Curiously, Jill had felt no compulsion to ask any questions of her own, not even the company name or her interviewer's. But neither had she felt any apprehension, not even any curiosity, really. The voice had filled her with trust and confidence. And back in the far recesses of her mind, from her mental perch, that place where we watch ourselves and monitor our behaviour, she'd watched this experience transpire, and she'd wondered.

Jill crossed another street and with a sigh of relief spotted an old three-storey brick building with a small engraving on the front that identified it as Sloan Hall. That matched the name she'd been given last night.

Just before she'd hung up last night Jill had been startled out of her somnolence by the voice asking her again, "Jill? Can you answer my question now? How much you want this job?"

She'd answered right away, without actively thinking about it. "I want it with all my heart." She giggled in embarrassment, it was such a stupid answer, something a twelve year old girl says about a kitten, not the kind of response you give in a job interview. And it was absolutely true: suddenly, getting this job was more important to her than anything else in the world; she couldn't wait to begin. Her answer had seemed to please the voice a great deal; she could feel his smile through the phone line, sense the satisfaction. "That's just what I thought, Jill. We'll see you tomorrow. Sleep well."

Sleep well. Well, she'd done that, alright.

*   *   *

GARY PICKED up another stack of papers and helplessly looked around the room. There was nowhere to put these, either, and the lab — hah! What a joke, more like *closet* — was just as messy now as it was when he'd started organizing the paperwork an hour ago. Except then he'd had some empty shelves and now he had nothing but floor space, and half of that was covered with equipment and God Knows what else.

There was barely enough space for two chairs and a desk. The room wasn't so much small as it was stuffed to the brim. Metal shelving units competed for space with overflowing filing cabinets and boxes of paper. The desk itself was huge, one of those green metal behemoths from the sixties, two yards wide and at least one across, and, like the rest of the office, buried under a foot of paper. Pamphlets, reports, files, looseleaf, photocopies, sheafs of magazines and documents of all kind, some going back fifty years or more.

Try as he might, Gary could find no consistent theme in all the paperwork he sorted through. Data from experiments on crowding rats into small cages lay beside reports on the space shuttle explosion. Psychology, physics, anthropology, every scientific field was represented. Cryptic notes scribbled in margins and pages of handwritten observations indicated a lone individual working on all these studies but betrayed no clues to the author's identity.

Gary thought he spotted a thirty-year-old electro-spectrometer in a corner beneath a box of microscope lenses. That could go, he thought. There's no way we'll be using that for anything like psych testing. At least, he hoped not. You never knew what kind of quack you were going to end up working for these days; Gary had no idea because he'd stopped asking questions after he'd heard the salary. As long as he didn't have to kill anyone he was being way overpaid. *Hell,* he thought, *even then I'd still be overpaid.*

Gary moved a stack of papers off an ancient brown coffee machine (he wondered absentmindedly if they still sold filters for that model) and set them to the side on the floor. He groaned as he straightened up and painfully stretched out his arms. His surfer's tan hadn't faded much in the last two weeks; his blond hair was bleached by the sun but the stubble coming in on his chin looked much darker. Instead of making him look unkempt, however, it added just enough age to his face to make him look somehow experienced. Not mature, but a bit less wet behind the ears.

Although leaving Santa Cruz was a big decision, Gary took the job when it was offered without so much as a pause. Moving across the country and finding a place to live had taken only two weeks, all of Gary's expenses paid in advance by his new employer, deposited directly into his bank account.

What the hell, he thought, *Give it a shot on the east coast.* He wasn't getting anywhere in California. Recently, the only lab jobs he could find were computer related, and Gary's qualifications in I.T. were non-existent. So far, he was the best educated clerk at the local Blockbuster outlet. He wondered where all the other psychology grads worked.

Nor did he have any personal relationships to hold him back. Displaying remarkable synchronicity, his love life and his career had matched their rate of decline perfectly. His demurral when offered a junior administrative position had been the motivating factor behind his last girlfriend's departure and he had accepted her departure as the necessary price to pay to pursue a life of research. But it was 18 months since he'd found work in his field, and he was starting to question the wisdom of his asceticism.

Besides, he'd always wanted to live through an east coast winter. The image of shoveling snow on a chilly winter morning hovered romantically in his mind.

Gary couldn't associate winter with discomfort – all his frosty experiences had been celluloid: Bing and Bob in Alaska, Kurt Russell fighting aliens, Jack Nicholson babysitting an empty hotel. He had yet to start a cold dark morning swearing in frustration and pain as his fingers slowly froze while he scraped frost off his windshield with a car key.

For the money this job paid, though, he'd move to Antarctica if required. Might as well get rich now. California would still be there if he ever wanted to return.

Gary straightened up with an armful of 40-year-old magazines and whacked his head into an open filing cabinet drawer. The searing pain from the collision burned down through his brain and caused his arms to jerk apart, dumping 74 copies of *Perspectives in Psychology* around his feet. Gary caught himself from tumbling over and as he hoisted himself erect he shifted his full weight onto his right foot, which shot out beneath him off the May, 1955, issue of *Modern Anthropologist*. As the floor rushed up to meet him, he determined this was going to be a long day.

Laying there, staring at the ceiling as the waves of pain subsided, he hoped he'd meet his employer before the subject showed up; one page of written instructions wasn't much to base a whole job on – two jobs, if he counted the subject's as well. And this office was a sty.

What sort of schmuck could work in a cluttered cubbyhole like this, he wondered, then realised that *he* was now that schmuck.

The thought did nothing to improve his mood.

*   *   *

"OH MY God, am I in the right office?"

Gary snapped his head around at the sound of Jill's voice. She stood in the doorway, one hand on the doorframe, slightly flushed from hurrying, breathing hard, chest rising and falling rapidly, ponytail bobbing behind her. And Gary knew, taking in the picture with a silent internal gasp of delight, he knew immediately that this was the best job in the world.

"Yeah, that's exactly what I thought when I got here this morning," replied Gary with a broad smile. "But at least it's got a window." He gestured over his shoulder; a thin sliver of light bled down from small pane of glass high on the wall.

"Oh, is this your first day?" asked Jill. "Maybe I'm not in the right office, after all. Is this 2C? For the lab work?" Jill started ruffling around in her purse, looking for the envelope she'd scribbled the address on last night.

"You've got the right office alright," answered Gary, putting down a dusty stack of papers on his chair. He wiped his palm on his trousers then extended his hand, "My name's Gary. We're working together on this project."

Jill ignored his gesture, slowly turning in a circle while she took in the maelstrom of paper that surrounded them. She looked shell-shocked. "We're working *here*?"

"Yup. Psych lab. You're the subject."

Jill snapped to life. "The *subject?* Oh, that's even better. I *at least* wanted to work with the data, not be a fucking guinea pig."

"It's not like that," Gary said quickly. "It'll be collaborative; it wasn't until I arrived this morning that I found out myself what we're doing. It's all written here." He picked up a page torn from a yellow legal pad; it was covered in neat, tightly-packed handwriting.

"Did I remember to mention," he paused slightly, "that I'm Gary?"

Jill took the paper from him then looked up just before the wry smile disappeared from his face. The anger vanished from her eyes and she visibly softened, a friendly smile lighting up her face.

"Sorry. I'm Jill. I'm glad to meet you. Really. I'm sorry I came on like such a bitch. I was disappointed."

It's amazing, this effect I have on women, thought Gary.

*　　　　*　　　　*

JILL BALANCED her coffee cup on the firmest looking stack of papers on the desk, pulled out a honey-glazed from the box, and directed a finger at Gary. "So you're telling me," she continued between bites and sips, "That we're working for someone we haven't seen, without direct supervision, without a deadline, without even any specific goal in sight."

"Yep," replied Gary, refilling his coffee cup. He had unearthed a box of coffee and filters and was pleased that the ancient machine worked perfectly; the donuts he'd brought with him this morning from a shop down the street. One thing about small college towns: lots of donut shops. "Looks to me like research for research's sake but who am I to complain? We're probably nothing but a justification for a line in somebody's bloated budget. If they don't spend it, they lose it – you know how it works. What difference does it make? As long as The Professor doesn't storm in and make our lives hell I don't care if he's a fugitive from justice even. This office leaves a bit to be desired but it's nothing if not cozy. And hey, don't forget the window."

They both looked up at the square of glass set high in the wall. It may well have been part of a much larger opening, but the presence of a mammoth, jam-packed bookcase below it rendered the possibility moot.

"I must have lost my mind," Jill said ruefully. "I can't think of any other explanation. Yesterday I had a great job with a beautiful office and for no good reason at all I've gone and quit for" — she gestured with her eyes at the overstuffed room — "for... *this.*"

"It was an ad agency," she said, responding to Gary's unvoiced question. "I called them last night and quit on the spot. I can't believe how understanding they were; they think I'm crazy, too. And they're probably right.

"I thought I was on my way to the big leagues, L.A., Manhattan, Madison Avenue…. I would have laughed in your face if you'd suggested I'd give it up to work in some little podunk lab. The only reason I majored in Psychology was because I want to know how people *think* — what better training can you think of for a career in advertising?

"*Now* look at me." She took another bite and chewed slowly, carefully, as if deciphering a complicated riddle.

"The really strange part about it, though," she continued, pensively, "is that I still want to work here. I mean, I feel really happy."

"I'll drink to that," replied Gary, lifting his coffee cup. He noticed her mood was slowly improving.

"Say, I've got a question," said Jill. "What makes you think that *you're* not the subject? This page of instructions isn't addressed to either of us."

"No, but the envelope it came in," Gary paused while he stooped over and pulled a torn envelope from the wastebasket, "was addressed to me, as you can see."

Jill leaned over to look closely at the envelope, checking to see that the handwriting was the same as in the note. Abruptly she pulled herself back, embarrassed. "I'm sorry. I didn't mean to imply that you'd…. I just, I don't know, I thought maybe there could be a mistake."

"Don't worry about it. It's natural to check," Gary replied casually. "Why don't we get to work?"

December

Jill sat as still as she could, arms flat on the desk in front of her, eyes locked on Gary's, staring and not saying a word. The effort she was making was obvious: damp forehead, clenched jaws, laboured breathing. Gary stared back, but without effort or concentration. He was merely a passive participant, and the last three months working with Jill had taught him the discipline to watch and listen without trying to help her.

He leaned back in his chair, smiled without taking his eyes off hers, and spoke in a quiet monotone. "OK, Jill, I think that's enough for now. Why don't we come back to this one later?"

Jill broke her gaze almost immediately. "Good…. Good." She looked down at the desk, at her knees, at her fingertips. She brought up her hand and pressed her fingers against her closed eyelids. "Wow. I was really trying with that one."

"I know, and I wish you wouldn't. You're supposed to let the thoughts flow naturally, without effort, just daydream, that's what The Professor said." Gary gestured off to his right, indicating their list of instructions, the only information they had ever received from their employer.

The List had taken on almost biblical significance for them, twenty-two lines of instruction read, reread, interpreted, studied and second-guessed time and again. It was taped to the back of the office door, which happened to be the only vertical space in the room not obscured by shelving or bookcases.

"That's *not* what The Professor said, all he said was 'Relax. Do not try too hard.' Where do you get *daydream* out of that? And why don't we even know his stupid name, I *hate* calling him 'The Professor' like we're on a TV sitcom!"

Gary could see that Jill was on edge; concentrating so hard for thirty minutes at a time was wearing her nerves raw.

Three months ago she was a lot more happy-go-lucky, finding the work fun, even. The assignment had been shockingly simple: Gary would look at cards with symbols or pictures on them and Jill would read his mind. That's it. Write up the results and do it until you're told to stop.

It was a joke assignment; Gary was probably right when he suggested they were just an excuse to help justify a budget. But they'd decided right at the start that their work, regardless of their employer's motives, would be completely professional. They kept meticulous records and observed every scientific protocol they had ever learned. Every Friday they faxed to their employer a summary of the week's results. They received no further instructions, no comments, no feedback; if not for the direct deposits of their wages into their bank accounts every week, they might have wondered if anyone knew they still existed.

The first month had been a breeze. They alternated periods of mind-reading with office cleaning. By the end of the month a few hundred pounds of paper had been sorted, classified, and filed. Problem was, there were still too many documents for the shelves and filing cabinets. So they carved themselves out a comfortable space surrounded by walls of paper and forgot about cleaning.

Jill guessed a card right every so often, but she couldn't mind-read for more than a half hour or so before she needed to rest. At first they tried to switch between half-hours of work and rest, but then noticed from their research that the longer the break, the better Jill's subsequent performance. This helped to rule out happenstance and random chance in her responses and after that they started to take their work more seriously.

They scoured their data for indications of favourable conditions or unusual responses; Jill's attitude to the experiments changed noticeably, from outright skepticism to great seriousness. They scheduled her tests for four specific times in the day and limited each to a half hour. The rest of the time they tabulated their data, interpreted the results, and wrote up their reports. They were partners in the experiments and partners in the scientific research. But only Jill would try to mind read.

Jill would have enjoyed relaxing for a change, letting someone else's brain search for images in the ether — that's how she conceptualized it — but the instructions were precise: Gary pitches, Jill catches. The participants never changed roles.

But that was just about the only clear instruction they had gotten; the rest of their duties they were left to infer from vague statements of policy jotted on their list: "Professional standards of research", "Exhaustive study", and Jill's personal favourite, "Controlled conditions" (this they achieved by closing their office door, disconnecting the phone — which never rung anyway — and turning off all the lights but one, a small banker's lamp with a dark green shade that sat off to the side on the desk). Their only prop, left by their absentee employer: a box of about five thousand flash cards depicting a range of images from simple geometric shapes to detailed pictures of animals and complex machines.

They made progress in their experiments. At first they were surprised and puzzled when Jill guessed about one in fifty right; by their second month she was getting one in ten right. And now, three full months after they'd started, she was right two out of three times. Out of five thousand cards.

*   *   *

SOMETIMES GARY thought he could feel Jill in his mind, tickling in places he couldn't identify. He wanted to turn around, deep inside his head, to see her there peering away at his psyche, delving into his thoughts. Just once he wanted to experience fully her presence in his soul, he wanted to share her the way she had him every day. But as much as he tried, he never could. She was always just out of reach.

Jill, for her part, loved the new sight she had discovered. Her mind was filled with vistas of unknown origin, paintings she had never seen and music she had never heard, but which she *knew*, knew in her soul, as well as you know your own name or the sound of your breathing.

She reached out with her mind, saw nothing with her eyes and didn't know it. She flew through corridors of light, swam hazily down tunnels of sounds and flavours and smells that came from someone else's brain, not from her own! The change had been rapid and her progress overwhelmed her. She focused her mind now without willing it, without thinking about it; the thought patterns formed themselves, wove a network of information and emotion, memories swept over her in waves, and then she would collapse and they couldn't work for hours. In those times Gary would hold her close or rock her in his arms, she was insensate but she demanded the comfort he provided, she needed to get close to the mind that had offered up such intimate images.

It was inevitable that they would become lovers.

FEBRUARY

Winter can be brutal in the northeastern United States. In bad years, February snowstorms are often followed by a week of sub-zero winds and freezing rain. This was one of those winters.

Gary had newfound affection for his car, a joke by almost any standard: 1976 Gremlin, no rust, but plenty of dents. At least the heater worked. And the beast was dependable. Gary couldn't suppress a chuckle as he drove past a shiny late-model sedan crapped-out on the side of the road — a note scrawled on a page from a daytimer flapped beneath a windshield wiper blade; a thick layer of snow was rapidly accumulating on the car as it lost heat to the frigid night air. The Gremlin might look like crap, but it started every time. That made up for a lot.

It hadn't taken long for Gary to adapt to his new environment. He carried a shovel, bag of sand, blanket and beeswax candle in the trunk, always prepared for the worst, even if that meant sleeping in his car. He'd fallen victim to a malady commonly affecting recent west coast transplants: overreaction to weather conditions. Just as tourists in Texas drive in fear that every other driver on the highway carries a six-shooter under the seat and won't hesitate to use it, Californians spend their first winter on the east coast in a state of shock and disbelief, expecting before each snowstorm that they'll wake up the next morning and have to shovel out a path through the snow from a second-storey window. Gary's sister had moved to Toronto and wrote him once about a radio announcement warning people not to let their cats out, because their noses would freeze in the cold and they'd suffocate. He'd almost forgotten that anecdote but now the image came back to him forcefully: rigid limbs thrust out, icicles clustered on whiskers, jaws locked open in the icy rictus of death. Peering through the windshield past the wiper blades slashing across the glass, Gary wondered how long it would take for *his* nose to freeze in this storm.

Jill sat in the passenger seat and let the rhythmic thrum-thrump of the wipers lull her into reverie. She looked forward to skiing tomorrow; it was well worth the drive to Vermont. In her opinion nothing else in this country compared to Stowe. She was hoping Gary would fall in love with the place like she had. He seemed to be adapting pretty well to real winter weather but his exposure had been limited to short trips around town; this was his first taste of long distance driving in a blizzard. And he hadn't spent a day standing in line at the lifts yet, stamping his feet and clapping his hands to keep them from freezing.

When the weather had turned nasty they'd debated calling off the trip but in the end had decided to go for it. In his paranoia Gary had bought the best snow tires available (Jill pondered whether the rest of the car was worth as much as just those four tires; she decided probably not) and the car was running well. There was no reason to stay home.

Gary replayed in his mind images from the opening scenes of The Shining, endless expanses of snow and ice, one lonely road winding between the mountains. He hoped their lodge would be more friendly, at least. Jill accidentally picked up on the images and giggled. "Don't worry, there'll probably be so many people you'll long for a few moments of solitude. This is a popular place."

A few months ago he might have been put off by her easy invasion into his mind, but now he expected it. She could turn it on and off without conscious thought, and their quiet moments together increased in frequency as his mind filled the silence with far more intimate communication than mere conversation could provide.

That's the problem, thought Gary. *Any other couple would have been burning up the sheets long ago!* But in the seven months since they'd first met they had yet to consummate the relationship; Jill's intimate probing of Gary's frontal lobes had overwhelmed her libido, to Gary's dismay. His attraction to her had evolved in the normal manner for all men and he had never deviated from that course, but for Jill their relationship had developed within her mind on an almost purely spiritual level and lust had been a late arrival. Their affection was almost platonic. While they'd spent the night together many times they'd always drifted off to sleep after only a few minutes of gentle petting.

Gary was unable to change the situation, as Jill wielded irresistible powers of persuasion over him; he simply could not refuse her anything. What was for most men a romantic exaggeration was the literal truth for Gary. Jill could convince him to do — or to do without — anything.

But that doesn't mean I don't suffer, thought Gary. *After all, I'm not made of wood — at least, not all of me.*

He wondered how she did it; it wasn't hypnotism, at least no form of hypnotism Gary had ever heard of, for she didn't mesmerise him with her voice or eyes — she simply filled him with an overwhelming sense of trust and confidence.

That would explain the ski trip. Gary had been on skis many times before, but those times had all been at places like Lake Tahoe in California where the surfers trade in their boards for a weekend of high-altitude sunburns and kegs of beer in the lodge; Monday morning they're back on the sand dunes regaling the beach bunnies with tales of how they stared Old Man Winter in the eye and spit in his face. Gary peered a little harder past the curtain of snow beyond the windshield and wondered how high the waves were in Santa Cruz right now.

The Gremlin hit a small patch of black ice and skidded for a second before catching the asphalt again. Jill barely noticed; she'd driven through a lot worse. She glanced over at Gary hunched over the wheel, knuckles white. *Poor fellow,* she thought, *maybe I shouldn't have pushed him to come up here.* She'd hoped that this trip would snap him out of whatever it was that kept him from hopping onto her and ripping off her clothes and making mad passionate love to her, over and over and over. She'd had her share of weirdo boyfriends but none had ever acted so disinterested in having sex with her. It was doubly frustrating: she could persuade Gary to do almost anything, but she was incapable of rousing lust in him. *Let's see if Vermont can help me out a bit,* she thought.

"There's the sign," said Jill, pointing. "We're here."

*   *   *

IT WAS even better than she'd dared hope: you could probably fit five people in the bed quite comfortably, the fireplace lacked only a bearskin rug to qualify for a Playboy photo shoot and — the *pièce de résistance*: a huge jacuzzi tub, set before a wall of glass overlooking miles of snowy white mountainside.

They were going to have a *great* time here.

*   *   *

IT WAS even worse than he'd feared: the room was designed for nothing but sex; Casanova himself couldn't have created a more arousing environment. He thought he felt himself getting stiff just watching Jill move across the room. How was he going to keep his hands — or anything else — off her for the next two days?

Jill tossed her bag on the bed then pulled off her sweater, drawing it over her head excruciatingly slowly, twisting slightly at the waist, stretching her t-shirt tight against her breasts. She let her sweater drop to the floor then barely turned her head to look over her shoulder at Gary; and in that moment he knew this was going to be the best weekend of his life.

*   *   *

THE LIFTS at Sugar Face at Stowe use the latest technology available to today's modern ski resort. Microchip circuits regulate the speed, optical sensors monitor usage, and computer-controlled dampening machinery virtually eliminates excessive swinging of the chairs, even during high winds that shut down most other lifts. There are even little pressure sensors in the seats which turn seat cushion heaters on and off. The only thing the lift can't do is help the riders off at the top.

Jill stood off to the side quietly chuckling as two snowboard beginners tumbled off the chair lift and skidded to the side, bumping together and knocking each other over. They ended up ass-down in a small snowbank off to the side of the exit ramp.

A full day of skiing had left Jill aching and sore. She and Gary had barely slept last night, preferring instead to pass the time making love. They'd mated in every position she knew and even when they stopped to rest they couldn't keep their hands and mouths off each other. When dawn came they finally passed out wrapped together, and when they awoke three hours later the first thing they did was make love again.

Jill chalked up their extreme passion to seven months' tension wiped away in one blow. And though she ached right now like she'd been beaten with a lead pipe she couldn't wait to get back to their room and make love some more.

The boarders were off again, careening madly down the run. They were nothing if not enthusiastic, thought Jill.

"Last one today, OK babe?" she asked Gary as he came schussing up alongside her a moment later.

"Sounds good. See you at the bottom," he replied and pushed off down the hill.

Jill followed him down and smiled into the cold air stroking her face. Sex had been predictably awesome with Gary; she had wondered if she would feel his orgasms with her mind, and when she did it almost knocked her out. She was coming for the third time when his first orgasm hit her. Forget clichés about fireworks and rollercoasters: this had been a nuclear explosion within her brain.

Gary hadn't shared in Jill's psychic uber-sex, as she described it, but didn't need to; Jill was the most responsive and intuitive lover he had ever experienced. She felt his enjoyment with two perspectives, and let her own passion build on the excitement he found in her body.

Their skin was electric together. The charge set their nerves on fire and flooded their brains with endorphins. Like Jill, he couldn't wait to get back to their room.

They swooped to the end of the run and skidded to a stop just beside the ski lift. They were right outside the engine room and could feel the low-frequency throbbing of the lift motor; the clanking of the chairs as they swung round and into position provided a hypnotic counterpoint to the deep rumble of the machinery.

Jill heard somewhere off to the side the boisterous voices of skiers and snowboarders as they readied themselves in line for the next lift chairs. She felt suddenly overwhelmed, the energy drained out of her, her legs turned to rubber and she sat down in the snow with a soft *whump*.

Gary hadn't noticed; he was peering through the fading late afternoon light trying to pick out the best route back to the lodge.

He cocked his head to the side as the lift noise seemed to rise a fraction in frequency, like a motor shifting into a higher gear. The rhythmic clanking of the chairs seemed to speed up a bit, too.

He listened for a moment and tried to remember exactly what the sound had been a moment ago, but to no avail. The engine noise seemed completely normal now, and Gary concluded the high altitude was playing tricks on his over-tired senses.

He glanced at the skiers and boarders waiting in line for the lift; they obviously hadn't noticed anything.

Two skiers caught a chair and were hoisted up and away, skis dangling below them in a clutter of blades. The boarders who had tumbled getting off the last lift moved into position where the next chair would appear and apprehensively readied themselves for its arrival.

Gary looked to the side and noticed for the first time that Jill was on the ground.

"Jill, are you OK?"

He bent over and cupped her chin in his gloved hand.

He lifted her face and looked into her eyes: they were blank, unfocused; her face was deathly pale.

"Jill!" he said again, this time with some urgency.

He thought he heard the lift machinery shift again; the rattle and clank of the lift chairs sped up and one chair swung against something particularly hard.

The sound made him look up. He saw a chair swing into position where the two boarders waited. They grasped the rail and the chair lifted them off the ground.

It lifted them up faster and harder than they'd expected; they clutched at the chair to steady themselves but lost their grip and started to slip off the seat as the machinery accelerated again.

The unoccupied chairs pulling into position swung crazily on the cable; along the lift up the mountainside the riders were all desperately gripping their chairs and trying to stay seated while the chairs increased in speed and swung madly back and forth and from side to side.

Gary glanced over at the lift operator; he was frantically punching away at his console and the look on his face showed that his actions were having absolutely no effect. The engine kicked into a higher gear and by now people were screaming. The two snowboarders were dangling from their seat and had already risen far too high to drop off safely.

The cable snaking its way up the mountain was dotted with bobbing bundles of flailing legs, arms, boards, skis. Various paraphernalia spun off the dancing shapes: gloves, hats, goggles, and the occasional ski pole peppered down into the snow from the lurching chairs. The engine screamed higher, the chairs at the bottom were smashing into support pillars, people in line scattered into the snow and the cable ripped through the wheelhouse.

And then it stopped.

It stopped completely and immediately. And as Gary stood there and watched, the two snowboarders were flung full speed off their chair and directly into the face of a support tower. They bounced off it and disappeared into the snow and trees below, leaving only a massive red stain across the tower where they'd hit.

Gary looked down and saw that the colour had come back into Jill's face, her eyes were focusing and looking up at him clumsily. Gary knelt beside her. He was shaking from what he had just seen; off in the distance he heard confused shouts and angry voices calling out. Jill heard the shouts too and started to ask a question, but passed out before she could form the words.

July

THE SOFT tac-tac of summer rain pattering onto the roof of the Women's Health Clinic lulled Angela into daydreams while she readied the examination room. She was frustrated with her job and it showed in her appearance: her uniform was wrinkled, she'd stuffed her hair into a messy bun, and she hadn't bothered to wear any makeup. As a nurse practitioner she'd thought that by taking this job she'd meet a doctor or at least a cute intern (at this point, she'd even settle for a promising pre-med student), but so far her only co-workers were other women.

What should have been obvious Angela had completely overlooked, and she chose the college women's health clinic over the local hospital because she'd hoped that the academic environment would attract intellectuals. Maybe it did – she just wasn't looking for deep conversations with other women.

Most of the time she could forget about her personal problems, but today she was running an ultrasound on one of her pregnant patients; well, *that* was just rubbing salt in the wounds, as far as she was concerned.

Ah well, she sighed, *mustn't take it out on the patients.* She resolved to be chipper.

*   *   *

JILL PULLED back the bedroom drapes and looked outside at the rain. It wasn't falling very hard, barely more than sprinkles, really. She sighed; she liked the rain, but she'd wanted to rollerblade through campus to work today. Now the pavement would be slick — too treacherous for blading.

Absentmindedly she checked herself in the mirror as she turned around. Keeping her eyes on her reflection, she slipped out of her nightgown then stretched and bent over, keeping her legs straight. She watched closely as she straightened up and then twisted at the waist. *Hmmm, bust is firm, legs are smooth, and the butt's still pretty darn tight,* she noted with a smile of satisfaction. She turned a bit more and examined her full profile in the mirror: barely a bulge. Her fifth month already and she was hardly showing.

All the more reason to get some good exercise today, she thought. And since blading was now out of the question, walking would have to do. She checked the clock: she'd need to leave earlier to make her appointment on time. Gary was already up and out the door. He liked to get to the lab early and go over the previous day's data. He'd have the morning all to himself today.

Her ultrasound was scheduled for 10:30 am, leaving her plenty of time to shower and eat a huge breakfast. At 10:05 she stepped out of their apartment into the cool summer rain and walked off in the direction of the Clinic. If she'd rollerbladed she would have needed only just over 10 minutes to make the trip, maybe less if her usual luck held out. It was a standing joke between her and Gary: somehow Jill always made the lights. Whether it was kismet or something more mundane she had no idea, but when she bladed she always got all greens. The brake on her skates was practically brand new; she'd had few occasions to use it.

Jill kept up a brisk pace as she crossed campus. She gave barely a glance to the offices and storefronts that she passed; a year ago all these places had been meaningful to her by virtue of past associations. But these days the past meant very little to her; all Jill's thoughts now focused on the future.

She and Gary were as deeply in love as any couple could be. She shared his mind as well as his body and loved both with a ravenous passion; he found his pleasure in opening his mind up to her, granting her intimate access to his soul. Of all the millions of couples who used the term casually, they truly were soulmates.

Jill arrived at the entrance of the Women's Health Clinic and paused on the sidewalk, looking up at the windows of the building. *What future are you going to tell me today?* she wondered. She took a deep breath, walked up the front steps, opened the door and stepped inside.

She found her way easily to the right office and a nurse showed her into an examination room. Her nurse practitioner came in right away and helped her up onto the table.

"Now don't tense up; the baby can feel it, you know," instructed Angela in what Jill thought was an especially patronizing tone. "They're very active right now. They turn and stretch their arms and legs, it's wonderful."

The nurse continued prattling on as she lifted up the front of Jill's t-shirt and spread a clear gel on her stomach. "This is just for conductivity. It's very modern now. With our last machine you had to drink 32 ounces of water and hold it until after the test. But this new equipment doesn't require any preparation at all, really. Aren't computers great?"

Jill half wondered if the constant chatter coming from the nurse would interfere with the ultrasound. She looked around the room: it was small and clean, just a desk and an examination table and a huge array of what looked like brand new diagnostic machines off to the side.

"This is more than I expected from a campus clinic," she commented to Angela, who was hesitantly flipping switches on the equipment.

"Oh yes, we're very lucky," she replied without looking up. "This is the latest 3-D, colour ultrasound equipment available. We received it as a gift last month from an anonymous donor. It's a bit more complicated than the last machine," she continued, frowning at one dial with a glowing red light; she couldn't seem to decide what to do with it, then finally settled the question in her mind and turned back to Jill without touching it. "But it works so much better than the last one. You'll love it."

"This will transmit the ultrasound into your body and receive the echoes," Angela said, bringing the transducer down onto Jill's belly; it looked like an oversized computer mouse. The monitor hopped to life. The blank gray screen was replaced by a swirling palette of colours, shapes, forms. It was a Rorschach test on acid. Jill hoped the picture got clearer. From such sophisticated looking machinery you'd expect to get at least a recognizable image.

Angela moved the transducer over Jill's stomach and the shapes and colours swirled madly. Blobs of fuchsia and violet blossomed into view and then washed offscreen. Jill thought she could make out the outlines of a solid form tattooed with various shapes and designs, and then realised that she was seeing the organs within the embryo's body.

"OK… now there's the spine… you see here's the heart, you can see it beating, see, and right over here…." One by one the nurse pointed out to Jill the various organs as they took shape on the monitor then passed out of sight with the passage of the sensor along her stomach. From time to time the nurse would freeze the picture and take a measurement by clicking with her cursor at different parts on the screen.

"See, now this is the thigh bone…" *click, click,* and another set of numbers was added to the column forming along the left side of the screen. "And according to these measurements," the nurse squinted up at the column of data, "the baby is 24 weeks old. That should help you get your date firmed up a bit."

"Now let's take a look at the brain, shall we," and she moved the transducer over to Jill's right side.

At the end of a long violet ladder-like formation where the spine was growing, a large round image came into view on the monitor. A slight tick of static jotted across the screen but didn't obscure the technicolour silhouette filling the monitor view. The nurse shifted the sensor over slightly and started taking measurements, clicking the cursor at various points around the cranial structure. The tick of static got a bit worse and then was joined by another, and then by a couple more. In a few seconds the screen was dotted from top to bottom with streaking rows of static.

The nurse looked up and cursed under her breath. "Oh, just when I thought I'd figured this thing out," she sighed. "Well, we're almost done, I think we've checked everything we needed to."

She let go of the transducer and bent over the desk to jot down a few notes in Jill's file. As she removed her hand the transducer shifted a bit to the left, just as the image on the screen rotated slightly. The baby was shifting position and as he did so his head turned toward the sensor. Jill peered through the static and caught her breath; from deep within the baby's face two crimson dots came into view and suddenly blossomed, building on themselves and cascading into two large orbs, burning spotlights that slowly deepened then froze, as though the baby were looking at her, could see her through the camera. The scarlet eyes locked Jill in their gaze.

As deep as deep red can be, those eyes shone out at Jill, burning through her thoughts and her mind and her very soul: into the back rooms where she stored forgotten memories; into her essence; into the references and recollections and life experience that give each of us our unique identity, those eyes shone their crimson light. Her experience in opening her mind to accept others' thoughts was of no benefit to her now — never before had she felt such an intimate intrusion into her being. Those eyes held her in their grip, unblinking, unwavering, omniscient.

A shrill beeping sound filled the room as a system failure crashed one of the machines in the diagnostic array. A bank of red LEDs lit up on one of the units, and needles on two dials started madly chucking back and forth. The static on the screen now completely obscured the picture on the monitor, with the exception of the two burning scarlet points of light, which stayed fixed in position and clearly visible through the interference.

Jill fought to tear her gaze away from the mesmerising stare in the monitor but somehow she couldn't look away. Alarm buzzers from at least two different machines were ringing in her ears and she felt suddenly lightheaded; her vision collapsed in on itself as though darkness were closing in from all sides. Her sight was filled with the image onscreen.

She felt herself being pulled, inexorably sucked deeper and deeper into an inky whirlpool. She wanted to call out to the nurse, to ask her to please shut off the machine, but she was unable to speak. Angela was still writing observations in Jill's file and seemed completely oblivious to the noisy systems failures.

From another part of her mind, from somewhere beyond Jill's conscious control, she moved her hand out. She held her hand over the ultrasound sensor and it hovered there, just above her stomach, as if waiting for instructions. From a place in the back of her mind came the impulse and her hand dropped and swept the transducer off her stomach and sent it clattering onto the floor.

Everything stopped.

The screen went blank, the beeping terminated, the flashing LEDs went out and the static disappeared. Jill still had her gaze fixed on the monitor; she couldn't tell if it was just her eyes holding the image or if the burning red circles of light were simply slow to fade from the screen, but it seemed to her that their image lingered for a second after the monitor had gone dead.

At the sound of the transducer hitting the ground Angela looked up suddenly, then over at the silent machines. She seemed surprised. "Well, I've never seen it do *that* before," she said with a puzzled expression. "It must need to be reset or something. But I think we got everything we need. It's all on the tape."

She leaned over and ejected a videotape from a VCR attached to the monitoring equipment. "If you like, we can make you a copy." The nurse accepted the dramatic failure of the ultrasound equipment with the casual equanimity of one who deals with computer crashes on a daily basis.

Jill turned her head slowly to look at the nurse, then paused a second trying to focus her eyes. "Say, dear," said Angela, coming closer to Jill and looking at her closely, "You look a little pale. Have you had anything to eat yet today?"

"No… um, no — I guess that must be it," Jill lied. Her speech was thick, slurred; she spoke with effort. "I was in a hurry this morning. Didn't even get my morning coffee fix." She pawed through her thoughts, trying to figure out what had just happened.

"Well then, no wonder you look like something the cat dragged in! You're not being very good to your baby if you don't eat properly — and I'm not talking about coffee, either. I want you to go eat breakfast right now! I'm sure whatever else you have to do now can't be half as important."

"Um, sure…" replied Jill, still feeling a little groggy, as though she were coming out of a deep sleep.

After clucking a bit more over Jill and exhorting her to be sure to eat well every day Angela bustled off to tend to another patient. Jill sat on the examination table and took two deep breaths to clear her head.

Her brain slowly started to process the information Angela had given her. She was having trouble remembering what had just happened. There was static on the ultrasound… and something else, but she couldn't remember what….

Twenty-four weeks, she thought. *That would place conception at… Stowe. It figures.* Their first night together and she hadn't thought they'd needed any protection.

So much for the rhythm method, she observed wryly.

AUGUST

OUTSIDE SLOAN Hall the sun halfheartedly fought a losing battle with persistent wisps of New England mist that refused to burn away in the dull morning light. Occasional murky clouds rushed across the sky while far beneath them chill gusts swept along the streets, gathering up the occasional scrap of litter. A lone grey cat had the sidewalk to himself as he trotted quickly off on a mission, looking neither left nor right.

Jill and Gary's lab (they felt that to refer to their office as anything but a lab would diminish the legitimacy of their research) had turned out to be the perfect place for their work.

Sloan Hall was located on the periphery of the college campus and its other tenants were all quiet academics who no doubt were attracted to the building as much for the low rents as for the peaceful contemplative atmosphere. Their contact with the other occupants was cursory and superficial; it was the perfect location for those wishing to minimise their interactions with others.

Jill and Gary neither saw nor felt any of this as they sat opposite each other at their desk, readying themselves for another session. Four times a day, five days a week, for eleven months now they had been working here developing Jill's mental powers.

Gary struggled to understand the nature of the changes Jill was experiencing. He sought to measure her abilities as though he were recording the growth of paramecia in a petri dish. A month ago he had made a detailed graph depicting her performance and posted it over a faded spot on one wall; Jill had removed it the next day, unwilling to quantify her mind's abilities with such an inadequate representation.

She struggled to explain it even to herself.

She saw emotions in her mind, in swirling clouds of colour and heat and light. Her interactions with others were rainbows in her head. She understood the tedium her bank teller struggled through every day and felt the frustrated ambitions and stunted dreams endured by salesclerks and tradesmen. She reveled in the joy felt by students she passed on the streets who had just completed difficult assignments; she laughed along with children playing games in front yards and parks, rejoiced with newlyweds and mourned with funeral-goers.

She visited art galleries, where she would stand and stare at the scenes captured on canvas and bathe in the artist's emotions. She immersed herself in people's moods. The collective tedium of a boring play was oppressive, but the cumulative bliss found at the symphony was exhilarating.

*   *   *

FLOATING IN the dark amniotic fluid, blind to all but subtle changes in the scarlet atmosphere, deaf to all sounds but the one rhythmic pumping that he had always known, reaching out but touching nothing, his mind came alive.

A deluge of visions burst upon him, sweeping him up, overwhelming him; he flailed helplessly within the heaving cascade.

Undeveloped pathways and immature senses struggled to cope with the torrent of information that surged through him. Unknowingly he kicked out in shock; primal reflexes jumped in a frenzied convulsion of stimulation. Thoughts and emotions he couldn't process overwhelmed his undeveloped brain.

Lacking the synapses to process the information, his brain shut itself off from the new stimuli; the darkness enveloped him once again.

*   *   *

GARY HELD in his hand a card depicting a complex pastoral scene of horses and hounds and brightly-clad riders. Jill's perception was now so enhanced she could discern even the expressions on the faces of the animals and humans. She carefully described to Gary the image on the card down to the smallest detail. She left nothing out: if Gary saw it, so did she.

While Gary paused to record her performance in his notes, she let the thoughts go and collected herself in preparation for the next card. As Gary picked it up and held it in his gaze, she once again relaxed her mind and reached out.

That was when she felt his touch.

She knew immediately that *this* was not Gary. She looked into an unpainted canvas of a mind. A mind that was not blocking its thoughts, or repressing them, but actually had *none*. No memories, no experiences. She had never touched a mind so deeply lost in the void. She felt the mind recoiling from her, as though it feared being swallowed by Jill's psyche. It drew away from her and was gone.

"What is it? Jill, what's the matter?" Gary asked immediately. He could see her surprise and puzzlement but felt nothing from her mind. Her thoughts were always a mystery to him.

"It's — something's different, is all…" answered Jill. She didn't know how to describe to Gary what she had just felt; how do you describe falling into a pit with your mind, reaching out for purchase and touching nothing?

"You don't look well. Maybe we should stop here."
"No, I'm OK, really. Let's keep going, I was doing well."
Hesitantly, Gary raised the card and held it in his gaze.

*   *   *

THE NEXT time the flood came the tiny brain was better prepared. The thoughts themselves fed the growth of synapses to process them. Pathways formed to route images that undeveloped eyes had never seen, neurons coursed down bundles of nerves and stimulated clusters of cells that had lain dormant in humans since the species had come into being.

Without benefit of sound waves, symphonies played in his mind; bereft of light waves, paintings took shape and mesmerised him with their harmonies of colour and form; he relived arguments and lectures and laughed at jokes told in words he'd never spoken and cried in anguish at all the injustices of a cruel world he'd never seen. He wondered at the emotion Jill felt and bathed in the love she held for him.

October

ANGELA GOT off the elevator and looked to her right, then to her left. Was Radiology down past the coffee machine, or was that …? She sighed in frustration.

It was taking her longer to get used to her new job than she'd expected.

Right about now, her decision to quit the women's clinic to come work here at the hospital was looking to Angela like a *big* mistake. When the position in the E.R. had opened up she took it without thinking twice, and where had it got her? Lower pay, terrible hours, and much worse working conditions. *If there's a silver lining to this cloud,* she thought, *I sure hope it turns out to be that hunky Urologist in "C" Wing.* Otherwise this could turn out to be one big career blunder.

Still, it was better than enduring the ostracism she'd suffered at the college clinic after she destroyed their brand-new ultrasound equipment. Like it was her fault; maybe if they'd provided her with proper training she wouldn't have done whatever she did that had fried the circuits and turned the computerized array into a very expensive boat anchor.

She'd been happy to leave after that, tired of walking into rooms where conversation died with her arrival, replaced by hostile stares and cryptic comments muttered underneath her co-workers' breaths.

Angela spotted the room she was looking for. There was a tremendous commotion inside and she increased her pace. She recognised Jill immediately.

By now, half the machines in this wing were malfunctioning or already down and the operating room was in turmoil, looking for all the world like an ambitious Christmas decorating project, multicoloured flashing LED displays blinking frenetically from the machines scattered around the room. Shrill little beeping, pinging and buzzing alarms sounded from all corners, serving only to drive the assembled medical personnel farther into confusion.

Jill had expected this, of course, and hadn't wanted to set foot anywhere near a hospital; a home birth was good enough for her, and her midwife had agreed.

But neither had anticipated a breach birth, and now the only thought on everyone's mind was getting the baby out of its mother before it strangled itself on the umbilical cord. That meant a C-section and consequently a hospital visit.

She'd hoped against hope that this hospital equipment would be somehow immune to the interference she generated, but when they wheeled her into the Emergency reception area every pager within 50 feet had gone off immediately, prompting two dozen startled glances down at screeching pockets and belts and purses. The receptionist yanked off her headset and staggered backward clutching her left ear; the feedback screeching from the earpiece was audible across the room, keening jarringly above the crowd noise. The automatic door to the ambulance bays noisily sliced shut, then open, shut, open, providing a hissing background beat to accompany the timpani of quarters spurting from the payphone in the corner.

Fortunately for everyone concerned, an obstetrician was waiting, having been forewarned of Jill's imminent arrival when the phones still worked. At breakneck speed an orderly propelled Jill's gurney through the corridor and into the operating room, where every machine present recoiled at her arrival.

A lucky thing, too, for had there been no malfunctions the surgery would have proceeded apace, but while the medical staff dithered, practicing every layman's favourite form of computer repair, distinguished by the whacking of machines with fists, indiscriminate poking of buttons and frantic twisting of dials, Jill's baby righted itself in the womb. Angela, the only person except Gary focusing on the patient, noticed the baby's shifting position and alerted the obstetrician, who set himself to the task of delivering the baby the old-fashioned way.

The silence was what everyone noticed first. And it wasn't that they were awestruck at the emergence of a new human being from its mother's womb. For them, typical 21st century human beings, the miracle of birth came a distant second to the miracle of technology. What inspired awe and reverence among the humans assembled in that operating room was the fact that suddenly, at the snap of a finger, every machine in the room resumed functioning perfectly.

The obstetrician held up Jill's baby and smiled broadly as it suddenly broke the silence with a full-throated wail.

*   *   *

TWELVE DIFFERENT babies occupied the maternity ward at the hospital, but only one was accorded constant attention. Every visitor, every nurse, every obstetrician and even every new mother was irresistibly drawn to Jill's new baby. They crowded round, waggling their fingers before him, cooing and clucking in baby talk. The child took it all in with wide-eyed wonderment; he gurgled softly and squealed in delight at every new visitor.

Behind a glass wall gathered the tiny new arrivals' various friends and relatives, pointing and happily commenting to each other with quiet excitement. Gary moved up to the window; a well-dressed man with grey hair and silver-rimmed eyeglasses moved aside to give Gary a position opposite his son.

"That one's mine," said Gary to the stranger; he couldn't resist announcing his patronage.

"He's certainly getting a lot of attention," said the man, quietly.

"What can I say," said Gary, "He's obviously got his old man's charm."

The fellow chuckled softly and drifted away from the window. Gary didn't notice: he was wishing the nurses would move aside and stop blocking his view.

NOVEMBER

PAUSING IN the marginal shelter of a large recessed storefront, Jill buttoned up her sweater and suppressed a small shiver. *This weather is so unpredictable*, she thought. She peered down into the stroller for the fifth time to check that her baby was well wrapped and comfortable. *I should know better than to take a walk around the block without bringing my parka*, she grumbled as she resumed pushing the stroller. A gust of wind slammed into her at the next intersection and she began to shiver in earnest. A large raindrop slapped noisily down onto the hood of the stroller; a quick glance at the sky and she was wishing she had thought to bring an umbrella.

She reflected that Gary would be back from Boston tomorrow, and he'd probably have the job. After five years in this small town, she would miss it. She looked up wistfully as she passed by the costume shop, the site of her first real employment and her first real relationship — both tragically short-lived.

And now another job was ending, another door in her life swinging shut. At first, when the letter terminating their project had arrived at the lab, she'd been crushed. But now her mind excitedly ran through dozens of possible futures that stretched before her.

When she got to the far corner she hesitated briefly and peered into the window of a small café; it looked warm and dry and very inviting.

Breakfast suddenly seemed like a great idea.

Inside, the cafe was a lot darker than it looked from outside. Six little booths along the side of one wall opposite a long lunch counter. An old couple in casual clothing sat opposite each other in the booth nearest the front window and an old man sat by himself at the counter; Jill took the third booth in and parked her stroller beside her. The menu on the table was stained and creased. The cutlery was bent. At the side of the table was a small group of plastic containers whose only purpose could be to hold salt, pepper, sugar and various condiments, but they were so dirty that there was little outward indication of exactly what lay inside each.

None of this bothered Jill in the least and when the only apparent employee of the place appeared beside her table, bereft of napkin or glass of water, she cheerfully ordered a BLT on wheat toast and a coffee.

He disappeared off somewhere and Jill and the three other people in the restaurant were left sitting there alone. Jill sat watching the couple in the front booth and realised that they were completely silent, staring down at the newspaper spread out on their table, saying not so much as a syllable to each other. Their coffee cups sat forgotten in front of them. *Not much profit margin in that table today,* she thought peripherally.

She glanced over to the other patron, sitting at the lunch counter. Decent looking suit, at least from the back; judging by the hair colour, he was probably middle-aged or older. This diner, too, was deeply engrossed in his reading matter, directing his attention to a newspaper spread out on the counter before him. He took a small sip from his coffee cup and turned his head slightly to the side. A faint glimmer of light glinted briefly off silver-rimmed eyeglasses, then disappeared as he turned back to his newspaper.

When her sandwich and coffee arrived she ate her meal with quiet efficiency and when she was done she moved the dishes off to the side, opened her purse, took out a pen and smoothed out on the table before her a clean white piece of writing paper.

Dear Gary, she wrote, *I hope you will forgive me someday for this.*
The baby and I are leaving. We are going where we can develop our special 'gift'.
You don't share our abilities, sweetheart, and though you don't feel it today, in a few years' time you will surely resent our talents.
But I can raise our baby without jealousy, and I alone can give him the environment he needs to develop his mind.
I will never forget you, my love, but please don't try to find us. I don't want you to waste your life in a fruitless search.
I wish you all the happiness in the world. Goodbye, my darling.
Love, Jill

She neatly folded the paper in half and put it and the pen away in her purse, placed a ten dollar bill on the table, stood up and wheeled the baby stroller outside. She walked briskly back to their apartment, packed three suitcases of clothing and mementos, put the suitcases into the car, strapped the baby into his car seat, and drove to the lab.

*   *   *

JILL PUSHED the stroller into the lab and switched on the lights. She swung the door shut behind her and slipped her coat off, hanging it on a hook behind the door.

"Oh, would you please turn off those overhead lights, Jill. I really can't stand fluorescents." She spun around and looked into the lab. Sitting behind the desk reading a stack of Jill and Gary's reports was a neatly-dressed man with grey hair and silver-rimmed glasses.

"I… I know you…" she said, furrowing her brow in concentration.

"I should hope so, Jill. We've met many times. Oh, I suppose you just don't remember, do you?" His voice was mellifluous, liquid. "Please Jill, won't you turn off those overhead lights?"

She found her hand moving toward the wall, watched it flip the light switch, felt herself turn back around to face the man at the desk.

"Come sit down, Jill," poured the voice from behind a pool of light spread over the desk by the banker's lamp. The reports glared bright white as they lay in the lamplight; it hurt Jill's eyes to look at them.

She placed the baby in its carrier on the desk and lowered herself into the chair opposite the voice in the shadows, peering through the dim light at the man's face. The reports on the desk were reflected in his eyeglasses; she found herself looking at two tiny images of the desktop, seemingly freely floating in the darkness.

"I've met a lot of sensitive people in my life, but I never expected to find anyone like you, Jill," oozed the voice. "We're very special, you and I. We both possess talents that the rest of the world considers only in fantasy."

His speech was gentle and relaxed, and it seemed to Jill that his words momentarily hung in the air, and then slowly faded away like wisps of mist; when he resumed talking it was as though he'd not stopped at all. Jill felt as one drifting in a boat on a very calm, quiet lake, floating past the shoreline of his words.

"Sadly, Jill, I discovered my abilities quite late in life; I was already mature when I learned how to use my mind, far too late to develop my abilities to anywhere near their full potential.

"Of course," he continued, a bit wistfully, "I couldn't help but wonder what I could have achieved if I'd been trained when I was still young, so I set about hunting for others I could train. But I found no one, and thirty years of research served only to convince me that I was unique.

"Every person I interviewed, every case I followed up, they were all just a crushing disappointment. Not a single soul possessed even a fraction of the mental powers that I had found within myself.

"And then I heard from you, Jill."

She recoiled from the sound of her name; the voice turned it into an ice pick thrusting into her soul. It chilled her as it gouged deep inside her; she felt the hair on her arms standing erect.

"You answered an old ad; my project had ended in failure a long time ago," continued the sibilant monologue. "But when I got your name and number from the answering service I felt you, *here*."

He raised his hand and tapped with a pair of long, delicate fingers on his temple.

"And I knew, right then, that you were someone special. I felt you, Jill, right through your phone number. You were the one."

The old man leaned back comfortably. As he receded into the shadow his face became less clear and the miniature twin reflections of the desk were snuffed out. He ran his hand lovingly down along the arm of the chair.

"This was always my favourite chair, you know. I must have spent thousands of hours here, in this chair, reading, researching, studying. I've missed it."

He stretched out his legs and rested his feet on the desk. He looked around him and gestured expansively with his arm.

"When you called this was the only office I had available. I couldn't bear to delay the project, so I put you two in here.

"I'm sorry I wasn't a better housekeeper, organization was never my strong suit. But I see you've done quite a bit of sorting and filing. That's nice...."

Reclining in the shadows of the dimly-lit office the old man kept his eyes locked on Jill; his words were verbal smoke rings floating dreamily through the air, drifting aimlessly upward until they wove their way into her ears. If syrup had a voice, it would be his.

"You're so much stronger now, Jill. That first night we spoke you were a blank canvas. It took no effort at all to make you sleep in, to rob your energy. You're much more of a challenge now. I must say, I'm very impressed with your progress."

Jill felt herself sinking. No, not sinking — buried. Layer upon layer of darkness was settling on her brain, snuffing out her thoughts, closing off pathways. She looked down at the baby laying quietly in its carrier. A small impulse struggled in the back of her mind, tried to tell her to *GET UP!* She knew she shouldn't be sitting here listening to this voice. She listened more carefully.

"I felt your progress even more intimately than you did, Jill. I was there every step of the way, in the beginning, helping you, shepherding your mind along the right path. Making sure you waited until you were ready."

Ready for what? she wondered briefly, the question a superficial thought passing along the periphery of her consciousness before the growing darkness extinguished it.

"You were quite the challenge, too," he continued. "Keeping you and Gary from, ah, 'making the beast with two backs', shall we say, was almost beyond me. But when you were finally ready it was no trouble at all to make you ovulate early. I suppose some bodily functions are easier to manipulate than others, eh?"

Up up up up up uuuuuuuuppp! The little impulse kept fighting in Jill's mind. If she could just lift herself to her feet and walk out of here she'd be perfectly fine. Everything will be OK, she repeated. Just – get – up. Maybe in a minute.

"I hadn't anticipated, however, one little side effect of your pregnancy." A rueful tone crept into the velvet voice. "I hadn't expected you'd have such a strong effect on computerized machinery. I was absolutely stumped until you gave birth — then it all became clear.

"I'd been absolutely despondent, thinking you'd somehow developed the one attribute that could keep you away from me forever."

Jill looked up, puzzled.

"You see," he explained, "we all have our cross to bear, and mine is a little microchip implanted in my heart: pacemaker. God bless modern science, eh?" The voice chuckled softly but was every bit as oily smooth.

"And then," he paused briefly and dropped his gaze to the baby laying quietly gurgling in its carrier, "and then you gave birth, and your influence disappeared."

Both adults looked down at the baby; its eyes twinkled in the reflected lamp light.

The old man continued.

"I understand now what I had failed to anticipate: our brains, Jill, like every other animal's brain on this planet, operate on electrical energy; and every brain possesses its own unique electrical frequency. But because humans don't use their brains anywhere close to full capacity, the electrical energy we produce is far too weak to interfere with other electrical devices."

He smiled, and the dim lamplight glinted softly off his teeth. "Present company excepted, of course."

"The electrical frequency of your brain is incompatible with the frequency emitted by your child's brain. Oh, it's quite normal; you don't share the same blood — why should your brainwaves be compatible? And it's obvious that you both have exceptional brains. Together, in one body, you two produced an intolerable interference that played havoc on any electronic device you encountered when you were particularly stressed. But when you and your child were separated forever in the miracle of birth, that interference disappeared."

The little impulse in Jill's brain was not so little anymore. She could feel her legs tensing.

Yes, Jill, up we go. Walk out of here and we'll be safe. Just stand up, Jill.... She piled all her energy into obeying that command, she repeated the thought, *Up Up Up Up Up.*

When the motion came, nothing would keep her from getting up and walking out of this office *forever.* In a minute.

"Is... the experiment... over?" The words barely escaped Jill's lips; her eyes were clouding over; her muscles looked slack.

"Over? Well, for *you* it is, I'm afraid, my dear."

His inflection of the word 'you" was almost imperceptible, but she caught the subtlety through the fog in her mind and began to suspect what he was planning; her eyes widened slightly and she caught her breath.

"Hmmm? Oh — no, no, please don't be concerned, Jill. I could never harm you physically. That would be so... *neanderthal.*"

He stood up now and pulled a thick envelope from his breast pocket and placed it on the desk before Jill.

"That's your severance pay, if you will. $50,000, a passport and a plane ticket to Canada. Five minutes after you leave this office you'll forget you were ever here. An hour from now you'll think you're as Canadian as maple syrup. I'm sorry to say, you won't even remember *me,* Jill. Or...."

His voice trailed off as he glanced down at her child.

The impulse in Jill's head was strong now and she took refuge in it. She clung to it as her last lifeline, her hidden reservoir of strength. She readied herself to get up, to leave this man and this place, to — suddenly she looked up, looked into the man's eyes and she saw! She realised with a start where the impulse was coming from. It wasn't some deep, internal voice of reason or sanity — it was coming from inside *him!*

The urge to stand and run away was coming from *his* head, *his* thoughts. Jill wanted to scream, to tear at his hair, his eyes, but she could do nothing. He was invading every inch of her brain, overwhelming her thoughts and her will.

"At first, I wasn't sure how I could take your baby without causing all sorts of trouble," he continued, seemingly oblivious to the turmoil raging in Jill's mind.

"Gary's mind is weak, but he's nowhere near as susceptible to my thoughts as you are, Jill. You're a natural empath: your wonderful talent is also your greatest vulnerability.

"But I knew Gary would never willingly give up his child to me. My ultimate solution is quite elegant, if I do say so myself. May I have the note you wrote up this morning, please Jill?"

Without waiting for her to move, he leaned over and pulled the note out from her purse, then laid it on the desk, in the middle of the halo of light.

"He'll come back and find nothing but this note and he'll spend the rest of his life looking for you and no one will ever think to look for me. And as for this little fellow…" he gently ran his finger along the baby's cheek. The child looked up and gurgled pleasantly; tiny pink hands clenched aimlessly. "Well, I can't even think where to begin, but I hear they clone bulls with just a few cells from an ear…. I suppose that would be the logical experiment to start with. After that, he and I will have a pretty full schedule, I'm afraid. This quality of subject comes around only once in a lifetime, more likely never. I have a lot of tests to run on this little guy."

"It's time to leave now, Jill."

He made a slight upward motion with his hand and Jill felt herself standing up. "You may give in now to that impulse you're feeling to run away." He slipped the envelope of money into her purse and hung the bag on her shoulder; she didn't resist.

"I really can't thank you enough, my dear. I'll never forget you; too bad you can't return the sentiment."

He chuckled quietly at his own joke and backed away slightly to give Jill room to exit the office.

As he moved away Jill saw her right hand move over to the desk and pick up a small sharp message spike sitting beside the lamp. She curled her fingers around its base and brought it close to her chest.

Behind silver framed glasses the man's eyebrows lifted slightly in surprise.

"Why Jill — I'm truly impressed! A mother's love must be powerful indeed, to give you the strength to raise your hand against *me*." He backed away a step. "But I don't think even you can prevail here; put it down and *leave now*." Despite taking on a hard edge, his voice lost none of its irresistible compulsion.

Jill looked back down at the desk and began to lower the hand holding the spike. In the same motion she reached out with her left hand and grasped her baby's tiny hand in hers; without pausing she drove down the spike, point first, through her hand and through her baby's, impaling both in a gruesome red shish-kebab of clenching flesh.

The man's eyes widened in shock at the sight, and then clenched shut as the pain hit him. His chest ignited in a blaze of fire at the renewed connection between mother and child. He clutched frantically at his breast, grunted, and collapsed in a crumpled heap.

*   *   *

JILL PUSHED the chair with the old man's body out the lab doorway. She wheeled the chair a few yards down the hallway and unceremoniously dumped the body in front of an unmarked office door. Then she turned and wheeled the chair back into the lab.

She dug around in her purse with her unbandaged hand and retrieved a small cigarette lighter. She carefully picked up the note she'd written to Gary, held it over the wastebasket, and applied the flame to a corner.

As the fire climbed along the paper Jill's eyes focused on the tendril of smoke licking upward. She couldn't remember what was written in the note but didn't care either.

It obviously wasn't important.

As the paper was fully consumed by the flames she dropped the bit she held and watched it smolder then die at the bottom of the metal can. She looked over at the desk and spotted her child laying in its carrier.

And in her mind she heard a voice say, "I'm sorry I made you hurt your hand, mommy. But don't worry, mommy, you won't remember any of this. It'll all be OK, mommy, I'll take care of you and daddy. We'll be a happy family, I'll take care of everything…."

524
1873
712
67

time trial

CHAPTER 1

I WAS STARING into the last remains of my seventh scotch and water when my friend The Amazing Cosmo slid onto the barstool beside mine.

"Cosmo, my man! Why, I haven't seen you in eons! What the devil have you been up to, old fellow?"

"Easy on the 'old fellow' stuff," he mumbled as he stuffed his hand into a bowl of peanuts on the bar. "I'm feeling a little long in the tooth these days."

I drew back a bit and squinted my eyes, trying to size the man up. Unfortunately, just about everything I looked at was slightly fuzzy right then, but I could still make out that the man was looking a bit ragged around the edges. Not his clothing, that was fine enough, no… it was his face. He looked worn out.

The last time I had seen Costin Mosetti, known to the masses as *The Amazing Cosmo*, he and I were working the same hotel on Ayers Space Station. We alternated as the opening act for a washed-up lounge lizard who could still pack the house with the bluehair crowd. I was a stand-up man, and popular enough, but Cosmo was the real gem – he performed a magic act that made the hairs on the back of your neck leap up and burst into calisthenics.

He'd start out his act pretty innocently, maybe with a card trick or something simple, and then gradually draw the crowd in deeper and deeper, inexorably shifting from illusion to impossibility. His show stopper was a bit where he'd zap himself out of a tank of water into a steel cube suspended above the stage on a chain, and when they brought the box down and cut it open and Cosmo popped out, the crowd went wild, as the saying goes.

I was every bit as dumbfounded as the schnooks in the audience each time I saw the act. I couldn't figure it out for the life of me, and gradually began to believe that Cosmo really could control magical forces.

Of course, eventually the bubble burst. The moment came as we unwound over drinks late one night in the darkened lounge after a holiday weekend blitz: three matinees and six evening performances in 72 hours can eat away the resolve of even the toughest birds.

"You know, there's not really any magic involved in my act…" started Cosmo without any preamble, slurring over the rim of his glass. "That is, nothing that most people would call magic, anyways…."

As he talked he played with a small silver device, about the size of a pack of playing cards, spinning it in tight little circles on the table like a child's top.

"It's actually pretty sad, when you think about it: such an elegant piece of technology, wasted, wasted…."

He followed my eyes down to the toy on the table; maybe he was as anxious to tell someone his secret as I was to learn it.

"It teleports," I said quietly. "That's how you do it."

"Close, my boy! Very close! But that's still not it…." He leaned nearer, enough for me to wish he weren't partial to Merzonian dungberry liqueur. The grisly web of swollen red veins in his eyes throbbed with intensity, a pulsing neon net around the black holes of his pupils. His upper lip trembled slightly, jerking in frenetic little circles a cigarette that protruded from his cracked lips.

He had always seemed quite imposing to me, standing over 6 feet and wrapped in his trademark black cape, but now, as he leaned across the little table, he was only a tired, gaunt old man. His silver beard was dull gray, and in the low light his skin took on the appearance of parchment, yellowed and cracked.

When he spoke, it was no more than a whisper, and my pulse quickened as I strained to catch his words.

"It's a *time* machine, my boy. It doesn't send me through space – it sends me through *time*." He said the word 'time' with an awful inflection, sounding like he was speaking of a living creature, an adversary, a colleague, anything but an abstract scientific concept.

"A time machine!" I exclaimed, probably a bit too loud. I quickly looked around the lounge; we were quite alone.

Lowering my voice to match the hush in his, I spoke with intensity, excited by his revelation. "But we know how time travel works – and the incredible amount of energy required to send just one atom back through time is enormous! That small box couldn't possibly generate enough power to send even your little *finger* through time."

"Ah yes, the layman's understanding of time travel. And I am happy to report that you are absolutely correct, but only within the terms that our scientists have chosen to frame the issue. It's true that vast amounts of energy are required to send an atom back in time even just one year; we resigned ourselves long ago to the conclusion that man will never be able to travel back in time to change history.

"And didn't the world breathe a sigh of relief when that news was reported."

He paused to inhale deeply on his cigarette; the glassite briefly glowed blood red at the end of the tube, then slowly darkened to a smoldering ash gray. As he exhaled, the smell of fermented dungberries that filled the air around us took on the soft flavour of fresh ozone. His voice was a bit stronger when he resumed speaking.

"But not all the data was released; The Administration neglected to reveal the results of short term transports over time periods of one to twenty-four hours. Those experiments tell a dramatically different story."

He spoke a little more quickly now, energized by his act of revelation. The colour came back into his face, especially in his cheeks and the end of his nose.

"But *I* have the missing data, my boy. My nephew worked on the original temporal project in the thirties and sent me a birthday greeting just before the time labs on Callnus were destroyed."

"Ah, right, the eruptions of Mount Esperus," I said, remembering the news vids.

"If you say so," answered Cosmo. "I thought so, too, but my system started acting up about six months after my nephew's birthday message; at first I thought it was a virus in the message, but in the course of purging the demon I found a hidden file buried in its metadata. It contained the full results of all the temporal experiments."

Cosmo paused again but I said nothing; he had my full attention. The silence hung heavy around us, broken only by Cosmo's grating breathing and the pounding of blood in my temples.

"The research was impeccable. They had spent five years calculating the energy needs of every element in the periodic table, and then spent another five years refining the technology to send those atoms back through time. What surprised everyone on the project was the tiny amount of power required for short term jumps. One hour's jump needs less power than a shuttle uses to dock; the amounts rise exponentially with increased time spans, but one day's jump can still be handled by a one-ounce power cell. Like the one in this little device, right here."

As he said that, we both reflexively looked down at the silver toy on the table, now sitting motionless. In the dim light, I fancied that it gleamed slightly, emitting an eerie, ghostly glow.

I stared intently at the device, and it slowly lost its otherworldly aura, finally reverting to a plain, inanimate object sitting beside our drinking glasses.

"You can understand why The Administration suppressed the data and killed the research team," he said quietly. "Why, interstellar finance has enough trouble right now dealing with the time-lag problems inherent in simple multi-light-year transactions. Can you imagine the chaos if people started jumping back even just one day? System-wide collapse, I imagine.

"Fortunately, I have no such aspirations. My insignificant little magic act can't hurt anyone, and as long as the secret is safe with us…" – he paused to look meaningfully into my eyes – "Well, it makes a good trick, doesn't it?"

His eyes twinkled merrily at me, and I immediately saw he'd been having fun with me all this time. I blushed, momentarily put off balance by his compelling tale and annoyed at myself for having swallowed it.

Before I could say anything, Cosmo swept himself and the little silver toy up and away, bidding me a pleasant good night. A month later our contracts both ended and we parted, bound for opposite ends of the galaxy. I never thought I'd see him again.

And now, suddenly confronted with the man once again, his unlikely tale returned to me with vivid clarity.

"Cosmo, that's a business suit, not a performer's outfit. Have you left the business? And whatever became of your… ah, the –"

"My time machine, old friend?" he answered, smiling. "That's what you're wondering, isn't it? Since that night long ago, you've wondered if I was pulling your leg, haven't you?"

My expression answered him before I could stutter out any half-hearted denials, and he resumed speaking, although his smile now took on a distinct melancholy.

CHAPTER II

"**I**'M AFRAID my time machine is all too real, my boy. In fact, it is presently the source of great travail for me, and the reason which brings me here to see you today."

He had my attention now. I sat up straight in the barstool and tried not to sway.

"Have you heard of *The Impossibility Corporation*? It's been mentioned in the vids a few times in the last year or so."

"Sure," I replied. "Who hasn't? They're the guys who processed the Calderan Flu vaccine for the Antares Colony – and they did it in one day, when it should have taken six weeks just to ship in enough technicians to run the cultures."

"Yes," answered Cosmo quietly. "That was certainly a trick, wasn't it?"

"No joke. And I heard an unconfirmed rumour that they cleaned and polished all the statuary in the Sillestrian Monastery the night before His Eminence's surprise visit. Three thousand statues! In one night! Can you imagine?"

"It makes me tired just thinking about it," laughed Cosmo, but his voice held a note of anguish, like that of a cuckolded husband telling adultery jokes. He seemed to sag.

"Actually, my dear friend," whispered Cosmo, "You are *looking* at The Impossibility Corporation. It is composed, in its entirety, of myself."

CHAPTER III

"**L**ET ME START at the beginning, with my magic act that we both remember from Ayers Station. If you examine the act, you can identify three distinct tricks that could be performed with the aid of a time-traveling device."

"Right," I said, "*The Eternal Hat* – that was a good one – and the big finale, of course, where they cut you out of a steel box… and, ah…"

"*The Living Mirror*," prompted Cosmo.

"Yes, that's it. But I never thought much of that one: it was obvious you used a double, or maybe holo projection. I couldn't say which."

"You couldn't be farther from the truth," answered Cosmo smugly. "The so-called 'reflection' really *was* me: just after the bit I would jump back fifteen minutes and join myself onstage."

"Yow." I was having trouble grasping the timeline involved. My head was starting to hurt, so I drank some more Scotch. Hangovers I could deal with, but time paradoxes were out of my league.

"And it was that little maneuver that got me to thinking about what I could really do with my little box."

Here it comes, I thought, and tried to focus.

"It wasn't long after we parted that an opportunity came my way," said Cosmo. "I was hired to entertain at a private party held in the Royal Palace of Ob, on the Fourth Moon of Gamos. While at the Palace, I chanced to overhear a debate on a crisis threatening the Royal Family: the Queen Mother was dying, and her final wish was to see her daughter married.

"It's not as romantic a story as it seems, sorry to say, for the old biddy had an ulterior motive: if her daughter were still unmarried when the Queen Mother died, the crown would revert to her step brother's line, leaving the old Queen's descendants out in the cold. And it gets pretty cold on the Fourth Moon."

"I still don't see –" I began, but he silenced me with a quick wave of his hand.

"Just listen," he said brusquely, and for a moment a dark shadow seemed to cross his face. I felt a bit of a chill, and started to wonder where all this was leading. But the moment passed, and he resumed speaking, a little more slowly.

"There were enough suitors that marrying-off the daughter wouldn't be a problem, but one crucial bit of ceremony stood in the way: in all royal Ob marriages, a bolt of fine silk from the groom's family is interwoven with a similar bolt from the bride's family. The threads are very distinct, and every new rug's pattern is very complex, representing a unique new crest created from the combination of the two families' crests.

"The crux of the problem rested in the weaving of the rug: there exists no machine that can be programmed to weave the complex pattern used in these rugs, and to weave such a rug by hand would take expert weavers at least six months. The Queen Mother had at best a week before she would expire, and the cause looked lost.

"That is when I got my idea."

I watched him closely now; he seemed to pay very little attention to me, lost in his story as though he were recounting an old myth half-remembered from lifetimes ago.

"I went to the Royal Chancellor and explained that I, The Great And Amazing Cosmo, could create this rug in one twenty-four hour period, and all I demanded in return was a large room stocked with food and drink for 500 men, and one tenth of the Royal Treasury."

"One Tenth!" I exclaimed, almost shouting.

"Down, boy," he replied. "Ob currency isn't worth so much outside of their system. It amounted to only about fifty thousand Terras."

I silently calculated the exchange rate on the Terra; Cosmo must have expensive tastes – if I were lucky, I might make fifty thousand in the next ten years.

"But I still don't see how you did it," I protested.

"No? I should have thought it would be obvious by now. It took them three days to finalize the betrothals and to get the silks; during that time I trained with a Royal Weaver. Then I locked myself in the Palace's Great Hall with the new pattern; I wove all day, and at night I would gather the silks and rug in my arms and jump back 24 hours and then continue weaving each morning when I woke up. After only 411 jumps, the rug was complete. And still only one day had passed. When I emerged from the Hall, I immediately became known system-wide as a miracle worker."

"Amazing." It was all I could say.

CHAPTER IV

As I understood it, Cosmo was using time travel to increase the work he could perform in one day. A simple task, such as polishing 3,000 statues, required the least thought: he would polish one statue on the first day, sleep for a few hours, and then at the end of the day pop back and join himself as the day began, and work beside his former self, each man polishing a statue.

If he jumped back at the end of every day, after 2,999 jumps he would have 3,000 of himself lined up, all polishing statues.

Of course, when he started work the first day, all 2,999 of his future selves would be present, since each of them in turn, when their day's work was done, would jump back to the same moment on that morning. So even though they were simply "continuations" of himself, because he always jumped back to the same moment, he appeared as a group. When the work was done he simply stopped jumping back in time. And he would have completed 3,000 days' work in only one day's time.

More complex tasks required rigid scheduling. If a manufacturing process followed several steps, each step needed to be completed soon enough to allow the completion of all subsequent steps in the same day. He couldn't build a skyscraper, because no amount of preparation would enable its erection in one day, but he could build a rock wall five miles long: all he needed to do was to break the job into however many day-long parts the job needed, and every one of his future selves would line up and work together to finish the job by day's end.

"I thought I had it made," he continued. "I did a couple more small jobs, time-sensitive, labour-intensive, low-tech stuff, and then I noticed in the mirror one day how old I had become.

"Because of the jumps, I was aging as much as one or two *years* in a single day, every time I did a job."

"If that's so," I responded, "You should be dead from old age by now."

"Yes, you'd think so, but remember that I still had all the original data from the temporal project. I started searching for answers to my problem, and I found what I needed. Fifteen test jumps run in an auxiliary chamber, in a process which buffers the reconstruction data using information stored over a twenty-four hour period."

I suppose my blank expression tipped him off, for he continued, "What that means, my dear fellow, is that I no longer have to jump back and grow another day older, but rather, I can jump back into a body that is twenty-four hours younger, the exact replica of me, as I existed when the data was originally stored."

"Which means, time stands still for you?" I asked, incredulous. "So this new method allows you to repeat any day as often as you want, without aging? It sounds incredible!"

"The only stumbling-block involves the brainwave data; that's why the experiments never gained prominence in the main project. The new temporal method can reconstruct enough of the original brainwave patterns to carry forward the last day's memories, but beyond twenty-four hours it breaks down. Jump back a day and a half, for instance, and you'll find yourself standing in a strange place, wondering where and who you are."

I was feeling that way right now, anyway, but I sat mute and listened.

"So I kept the jumps down to 24 hours and I thought I'd solved all my problems, but unfortunately things just got worse."

His eyes sparkled malevolently in the lights reflected from the bar. "I've done twelve jobs in the last five months, and worked a total of 27,000 days."

I gasped. "Twenty-seven thou–"

"Let me do the math for you," he said softly. "It works out to about seventy-four years."

"But why?" I asked. "Why not retire? You must be absolutely loaded by now."

"Hah. You'd think so, but these things have a way of getting out of hand. I have so many investments now and my hand in so many multi-system businesses, I can't retire without bringing half the galaxy down on my ass. Why, already I have several additional commitments pending, spanning dozens of systems."

"That's tough, Cosmo," I said, leaning back in my chair. I was starting to get an inkling of what brought Cosmo to belly-up to this bar tonight. "So…" I went for the pregnant pause to affect an air of unconcern, "How can I help you out?"

"Ha! That's just what I was hoping you'd ask, my boy!" responded Cosmo with more enthusiasm than I'd expected.

"But I've not come here to get you to 'help me out', as you so generously suggest, but to ask you to become my partner. That's right, a full partner, at least in tonight's job, and tomorrow the whole thing will be just a memory, except for the money in your pocket.

"I've got everything ready – I've rented an orbiting science facility for tomorrow. Just let me explain how it works, and we can get underway…."

CHAPTER V

I WAS STANDING in a big room. And in that room were at least two thousand men, all of whom looked exactly like me. Because they were me. Still are, for that matter.

One of them strode out and extended his hand to me. "Welcome aboard! First day, isn't it?"

I was having trouble grasping the weirdness of talking to myself – quite literally! – despite having been well prepped. Luckily, my double was understanding, and gently took my arm, saying, "Look, don't worry about figuring any of this out. All you have to do today is learn the lay of the land, OK?"

"Sure," I replied dreamily, while I gazed goggle-eyed at the multitude of me's before us.

"Think of me as your guide," said my friend, as he helped me into a white lab coat that he pulled from a hook on the wall. "Come with me and I'll show you the setup."

He led me through long lines of workers, some standing at counters, some working in little desk hutches, some of them operating machinery and others running throughout the complex, carrying supplies or equipment. It was a fairly unremarkable operation, except of course for the fact that every visible human being was identical in every way but one. And that one difference rested in a small white badge pinned on each man's left breast pocket where a number was written.

I looked down at my own chest – on my badge was neatly printed the number 1. I noticed my guide's badge read "15".

"How high do these numbers go?" I asked my guide.

He grimaced wryly and said, "Well, they didn't want to tell us at first, but I suppose they figured we'd be perpetually distracted until we found out, so they let us know that we top out at 3275."

"3275!" I exclaimed.

"I know," he said, "But now that we're here, let's get on with our work and make the best of it. We're not getting any younger standing here jawing."

We won't be getting any younger or older for quite some time, my friend, I thought as we headed off down past the endless rows of clones quietly toiling away at their stations.

We passed training rooms, but most had only two or three people inside; we passed deserted cubicles and conference rooms and came to a supply room where a long line of lab coat clad workers waited, with others already carrying out armfuls of items, scurrying off to their posts like dozens of snowy-white rats scuttling back to their hutches.

So far it all looked pretty straightforward, if you ignored the doppelganger workforce, of course, but when we got to the cafeteria I was really thrown for a loop. A few stragglers were scattered here and there still finishing their breakfast, and some kitchen staff were moving about preparing for the lunch rush.

But at the far end of the big room, past long, silent rows of folding chairs tucked in place against the tables, thirty or forty men were boisterously carousing and raising hell. A few of them were stark naked, and another had already passed out and was sleeping, face down, on the floor beneath a table.

My guide followed my gaze and twisted his face in disgust. "Always a few bad apples in a bunch. Those loafers ought to be made to pull their weight," he said angrily.

Our tour came to an end when we arrived at a long corridor punctuated with a door every few dozen meters. My host opened the door closest to us, which was marked '1 to 400', to reveal a huge dormitory and row upon row of bunk beds.

"This is where you'll sleep tonight," he said, pointing to the first bed, which was marked with the number "2".

"Always sleep in the bed marked with the next number up from what's on your badge; there's clean pajamas on the bed. Just before you go to sleep activate the time machine. It'll send you back 24 hours. In the morning you'll find a set of clean clothes at the foot of your bed. And a new badge, and your new number."

I looked at him dumbfounded. "I change beds every night? Where do I keep my stuff?"

"You don't have any stuff," he replied. "All you own is what's in your trouser pocket."

When he said that, I became suddenly conscious of the lump in my right pocket where the time machine rested. Instinctively, I glanced down at 15's jacket, and saw the same telltale shape bulging in his pocket.

"OK," I replied, starting to feel somewhat more comfortable. "Show me what to do."

CHAPTER VI

THE DAYS PASSED fairly quickly once I got settled in. The first couple of weeks I went to training sessions that covered every aspect of the manufacturing plant we were operating. Training sessions that my future selves were conducting.

After that, I moved to a new department every few months, advancing in seniority and skill day by day. I would be an apprentice one day, a worker the next, management a few weeks later, and then start from scratch somewhere else.

The last day I spent in any department was spent writing up a training manual for that skill which I would leave in the orientation room for me to read on my first day in that position.

It took a long time for me to overcome my tendency to view time in a linear manner. I still couldn't reconcile the fact that the skill and knowledge I built up performing any task I could pass back down to my various selves before they had even started working on those tasks. I suppose what Socrates said about all knowledge already being within us wasn't so far off from the truth.

Different departments started at different times, according to the gold extraction and molding process. Extraction and Purification started early in the day and were done by noon. Polarization came next and was done by 3 pm, when Molding and Polishing took over; those workers spent their days sleeping and reading, only to jump into frenzied activity for 3 hours every afternoon.

By 6 pm every day, the bracelet was finished and carried off to the front office, and I would drag myself off to bed and wake up one number higher, one day closer to completion, one day closer to freedom.

Some days were boring and some were exhausting. A few will haunt me until the day I die.

CHAPTER VII

I T HAPPENED on 813. I have no record of the incident but in my memory. I like it that way. Maybe someday the memory will go away, too.

It was a pretty normal day, and my first one as a maintenance man. They gave me a manual to study and left me alone in a room while seven others of me waited outside in the hallway, which puzzled me the first time through. There wasn't enough work for two of us, let alone seven – the plant was powered by an HP Home Fusion NucloJet, which hasn't got more than four or five moving parts. Not much to break down there.

At 10am the rest of them suddenly came in to the room where I was waiting and stood around expectantly. Nobody said much, and I couldn't help but feel that we were all waiting for something.

At 10:20 a red light on the fusion unit started flashing. One of the maintenance men approached it, scanned the message display on the unit, then walked over to me quickly.

"813," he said, quietly, urgently. His tone told me this was serious. "We have a problem. This fusion unit has to be shut down immediately so that a technician can replace the particulate matter exhaust chamber."

I was nonplussed. "And?"

"Before the part can be accessed safely, the reactor has to be shut down for several hours." He looked at me. "We don't have several hours." He looked at me some more. The penny dropped.

"Oh." What else could I say?

They wrapped me in as much lead as I could wear without falling down, and then practically injured themselves getting out of the room. I heard the telltale clunk as the reactor shut down and I had the cover off the unit before the echo disappeared.

It couldn't have taken more than 5 or 6 seconds to remove the exhaust attachment when I felt my skin starting to sizzle. By time 20 seconds had passed, my head throbbed with a thousand headaches and my vision started to cloud over in crimson sheets.

At the 30 second mark I had the new exhaust chamber in place but could no longer see clearly enough to properly reattach the unit's cover. I propped it in place, and somewhere around 35 seconds my legs gave way and I doubled over. As I tumbled onto my face, or what was left of it, I saw the door burst open and several rad-suited figures rush toward me.

One of the suits snapped the cover back into place while another rolled me onto my back and yanked off my helmet. I gasped at the rush of air, and moved my lips to speak, but no sound came – my cracked lips opened, and a thick, red bubble of blood slowly oozed out of my mouth and down my chin. My lungs were full of blood, but breathing was far too painful to consider, so it made little difference.

The form hovering above me reached into my pocket and pulled out the time machine. He pulled off my glove to put it in my hand, and I remember dreamily contemplating how pretty and ethereal the silver looked against the raw crimson meat of my blistered fist.

"Push the button," he said, urgently.

Even in my fatal stupor, I could hear the scream in his voice. And I would have obeyed, but everything hurt so much, and I just needed a moment to regain my strength —

"Push… the… button!" The man's urgent whisper was equally pleading and commanding.

"Listen. I can't do it for you! *Push the button!*"

I remember trying, I'll admit that. But there's just no way I had the strength to move my hand. I can't explain it for the life of me, but one moment I was laying in that room feeling the life drain out of my body, and then I was laying, curled up, in the dark fusion room. And I could breathe.

I lay there, rocking myself quietly back and forth, until I started to shiver from the cold floor. I stopped to take a long shower before crawling into bed. For the next 12 days I didn't do much but eat and sleep, and jump of course, every night, to lay awake in each new bed listening to the tortured sobs and ragged breathing coming from a dozen other men in the room.

I had sunk pretty low when one of me came in and sat down beside me on the bed. He had no number on his badge, just the word "Counselor" and a smiley face. The smiley face was such a ridiculous touch it made me laugh. At least this me still had a sense of humour.

"I know what you're going through," he began, and it occurred to me that this was perfectly true. "But we need you back. There's another three thousand of us depending on you. It's time to go back to work."

His eyes weren't sympathetic in the least, but he spoke with the calm assurance that can only come from having seen the future, not to mention having lived through every day of it. I trusted this man. I believed him.

He got up then, and walked away. I wanted to hug him, cry on his shoulder, make him my best friend. We never spoke again.

CHAPTER VIII

DURING MY 3275 days I got very lonely. It was Fate's cruel joke on me that the last real conversation I'd had with another human (besides myself) was with Cosmo. Cosmo's road-map eyes staring at me over a brandy snifter weren't exactly the lasting vision of humanity I had wanted to carry with me for nine years.

He'd told me about the job just before I went "in", and night after night I replayed the conversation in my mind, haunted by his asthmatic cadences and coarse voice.

"My client," Cosmo had begun, but then caught himself and looked me directly in the eyes and dredged up out of the deep recesses of his grey matter the closest approximation he could manage to a smile. If his nose had been longer I might have mistaken him for a crocodile. "I mean to say, *our* client is the Lady Pell of Tresha, which is the primary planet of Benera's Cluster.

"It turns out that the Lady Pell is the victim of a foul political conspiracy, a plan which required compromising the good Lady's reputation.

"A charming Captain in the Treshan Navy managed to seduce the Lady Pell, and during their last assignation, he removed from her boudoir an ornate antique snake wrap that she wears on her right arm. It is unusual in the extreme, having been crafted from Treshan Gold mined several thousand years ago.

"Have you ever seen or felt an object made from Treshan Gold? I have, but the experience cannot be adequately described, as the molecular alignment of the gold's atoms causes them constantly to shift polarity, ceaselessly twisting and flipping and writhing back on themselves. Imagine a solid object made of water – water which is in constant motion and yet still solid. There is no feeling comparable to wearing Treshan Gold."

"This hardly sounds like a challenge," I interrupted. "I'm sure the Lady Pell has the resources to have any idiot jeweler make a duplicate."

Cosmo sighed quietly, but persistently maintained what I'm sure he thought was a disarming smile. I wondered if I would be able to hear it when the tendons in his cheeks snapped like crisp rubber bands. He took another drink and continued in an even tone.

"Three days from now the five thousandth anniversary of Treshan independence will be celebrated in a formal ceremony held on Tresha in the Stellar Coliseum.

"And it is there, before hundreds of powerful rulers and planetary officials, that the adultery of Lord Pell's wife will be revealed: at a significant point, Captain Graxx of the Treshan Navy will present himself and his wife to Lord Pell, and the Lady Graxx will be wearing, around her right arm, the unique, unmistakable serpent, late of the lovely Lady Pell's boudoir.

"The implications will be obvious. And Lord Pell will have but two choices, according to five thousand years of Treshan tradition: he can ignore the adultery and skulk away to live in disgrace, or he can challenge Captain Graxx to a duel in which he will most certainly be killed. Either way, his enemies will be rid of Lord Pell."

"So the Lady Pell hopes to foil their plans by having you fabricate a duplicate. Again, what's so difficult?"

Cosmo looked at me sympathetically.

"Part of the problem lies in its scarcity. No native source for the metal has ever been discovered, and all existing samples were mined from an asteroid which landed on the planet millennia ago.

"When the Lady Pell discovered the theft, she immediately set her servants to the task of quietly gathering together other objects containing Treshan Gold. She presently has amassed several hundred items.

"But because the metal is so exceedingly rare, there aren't any skilled metallurgists who understand how to work with it. The techniques are recorded in various manuals, of course, but to train an adequate set of workers how to extract the gold and smelt it into a new bracelet would take months, if not years. Months and years she doesn't have.

"Consequently, this morning she contracted with me – with *us*, my dear fellow – to extract the gold from each item and to smelt it into a new serpent.

"I told her we would have one for her tomorrow," he added quietly.

"Another! From Treshan Gold! Tomorrow!" I had sputtered at Cosmo, overwhelmed by the concept. "That's absolutely impossible!"

"I know," Cosmo had replied. "That's why I accepted her request. After all, it's our specialty."

CHAPTER IX

O N **1733** I was sent to the training center, this time to act as an instructor. After spending almost 300 days in Polarization Control, evidently management must have felt I was ready to start teaching the technique. 1466 and 1467 straggled in, looking for all the world like galley slaves starting on a round the world cruise.

1466 looked around at the empty room. "Are there any more?" he asked.

"No, you're the only ones," I answered. I hated small talk with lower numbers; probably the only thing that can make chit chat more tedious is to repeat it, word for word. "Let's get to work. Polarization is complicated – this is a two-day course, as some of you already know," I added, looking up at 1467. He didn't return the courtesy, and sat sulking at his desk, looking at his fingers.

I sighed; this was bringing back too many unpleasant memories. At least in the labs I had my own cubicle and I didn't have to interact with myself.

"Here," I said, tossing a sheaf of papers onto each man's desk. "These exercises have been designed to teach you the set of steps involved in Polarization." 1467 was already flipping through his papers, skimming the questions; 1466 still paid attention. I sighed again. "Come ask me for help when you don't understand something. I'll be sitting right here. All day."

CHAPTER X

I SAW MANY accidents, cuts, burns, and bruises. Of course, I saw only lower numbers have accidents, so I could never benefit from the repeat performances, except to cringe sympathetically every time I witnessed each unhappy incident.

Group activities were virtually nonexistent, and almost any meeting of more than 3 of me was concerned exclusively with work-related matters. Solitary activities are the only tolerable diversion when three thousand men who can't stand each other share the same living space.

*   *   *

At 2000 I threw a little party for myself, and planned to spend the day drinking and laying naked in the cafeteria with the other carousers.

I was already half roasted when I noticed passing by, at the far end of the room, the new guy on his orientation tour.

As I lay there, trying halfheartedly and unsuccessfully to remember what he was thinking, I happened to glance at his guide's face. The look of disgust that twisted his visage left no doubt as to the nature of his thoughts.

"Just wait, asshole," I muttered. "Just you wait and see."

CHAPTER XI

From **2312** to 3044 I did the most difficult work, removing the final extraction of Treshan Gold from the samples.

2331 was my first day working with the smelters, and I was checking the operating manual when my unit overheated, splattering my hand and forearm with molten Treshan Gold.

If feeling a bracelet or pendant made from Treshan Gold can be compared to caressing an angel's wings, as I believe it has, then being burned by molten Treshan Gold must be fairly equal to receiving the business end of Satan's pitchfork.

The metal burned through my glove and skin and bone like an eruption on the sun. The hole widened as it deepened, as the liquid metal spread out and leapt along my bones and muscle tissue. Fountains of blood that spurted from the wounds sizzled into billows of crimson steam as the Treshan Gold incinerated the very air around my arm.

I felt myself passing out from the pain and was fumbling with my good hand at my jacket pocket when a fellow technician took my arm.

"No," he said. "Not until we get the gold back."

It took about an hour for the cooled gold to be cut out of my veins. The worst of it was, I couldn't take an anesthetic, as we couldn't risk my passing out and dying before I could wake up to press the button.

So I lay there, with four of them holding me down, while they scraped lines of cooled Treshan Gold out of my tattered arm.

Two of the men wept openly while the others cut me open, and another one of them cursed quietly with every one of my convulsions. I was too weak to walk when we were done, so they carried me to my bed, a solitary cot in a small little room, and watched me pop out before they left.

I lay on that cot for several hours then, screaming and screaming and screaming until my lungs were hoarse, and then, through the coughs and the tears, I would start screaming again. But by midday I was calm once again, and ready to go back to work. I had seen too much to fall apart now. No more visits from Mr. Smiley Face.

But whenever I happened to pass that room in the morning and hear those screams, part of my stomach would twist into a little ball, and I would have to hurry away.

CHAPTER XII

From days 3261 to 3273 I worked in the front office scheduling, coordinating and administering my 3260 other selves, and on 3274 I smoked cigars and walked through the plant smiling and nodding and confirming that every single detail had been dealt with and nothing overlooked.

Nobody smiled or nodded back, but I was feeling so good by then that I didn't care.

CHAPTER XIII

O N **3275** the first thing I noticed was the lack of a number on my new lab coat. I went directly to the door in the far wall of the front office and strode in, and found myself face to face with none other than the Amazing Cosmo.

"Cos–"

"Quiet, my boy! We can't have your other few thousand selves knowing I'm here – we'd never get a lick of work done if every one of you tromped in here when he was feeling lonely or bored."

"But what are you doing here? Have you been here all along – I mean…. Oh, damn, I don't know what I mean!"

"There, there, my boy," he said, soothingly. "I knew you'd be too excited today to be of much use, so I thought I'd drop by and relieve you of this –" he reached smoothly down into the pocket of my lab coat and retrieved the time machine – "and to pick up the bracelet, of course."

"Of course," I said, as the familiar sensation of distrust that Cosmo inspired slowly seeped into my mind.

"By the way, old boy," said Cosmo, as he fiddled with the time machine, lifting a flap on its front and punching some buttons; the display started flashing red and he casually closed the flap and looked back up at me. "I forgot to mention that you can also project a beam with this device, and transport something… or someone… while remaining in place."

He looked at me meaningfully. "I really do want to thank you," he said, "And I am truly sorry it has to come to this, but you would never accept another contract if you remembered working this one."

I must have looked panicked, because he immediately added, "Oh, don't worry, your next assignment will be much easier – mustn't wear you out too fast. Well, see you soon."

At that, he pointed the device at me and pressed the button. I had to rush forward to catch the device before it hit the ground, as it was suddenly left hanging midair when Cosmo popped away.

It felt especially warm in my palm. I looked at the display: Cosmo had sent himself forward 36 hours, enough to wipe out a significant portion of long term memory. I hoped he would still be useful for work, but decided that since he had intended to send me that far forward in time, it couldn't be too debilitating.

Cosmo was lucky I hadn't set the device to vaporize him, instead of just reversing the projection beam. I chuckled at his naiveté. How could he think I wouldn't have the time to play around with his device when it was the only diversion I'd had for nine years?

Ah well, I thought, back to business.

I put the device in my pocket and wondered if the Lady Pell was beautiful.

Did you enjoy this book?

If you did, then I'm delighted!

And if you'd like to see more like it, there's one simple little thing you can do for me that's worth its weight in gold (metaphorically-speaking):

Please leave a review!

Your online review will do more for me than you can imagine, and ultimately it will enable me to continue writing more books.

Plus, because I read every review, your review will help me to understand what you liked about my book, so that I can create others that you might enjoy even more!

THANK YOU, in advance.

--*J.M. Holmes*

Natalie Bernard is a Connecticut-based illustrator, working mainly in Photoshop using a Wacom Cintique tablet. She received her Bachelor's in Fine Arts at the Hartford Art School, and spent some time painting in Cortona, Italy, on scholarship.

Natalie's work can be found internationally on book covers, card games, and tabletop role-playing games. She specializes in fantasy and science fiction themes.

Her love for the fantastical stems from a childhood entranced by art galleries and inspired by the visual power that a well-written story provides. In her work, Natalie aims to tell a story with paint instead of words.

J. M. Holmes was born and raised in Canada and educated in the Classics by Jesuits and nuns who would likely be disappointed to see the results of their efforts.

A Renaissance polymath, Holmes has been the Editor of the bilingual magazine for Glendon College in Toronto; the Editor of that city's French-language newspaper, *Le Metropolitain*; a successful magazine publisher; and Director of the Davis Film Festival in Davis, California.

Recipient of the 2005 *Heroes Award* from the American Red Cross, Holmes has also received commendations from the U.S. Senate, the U.S. House of Representatives, the California Legislature, and the City of Davis, California, in recognition of extraordinary charity work.

Holmes is also the winner of awards in California for running a business with outstanding environmental practices and from Rotary International for producing that charity's weekly publication.

Sadly, Holmes bears some measure of responsibility for the overpopulation of Planet Earth, having participated in the creation of two additional humans, Alex & Sarah, both of whom are college students working hard at honing their skills in questioning authority and challenging conventional wisdom.

Currently, J. M. Holmes resides in the United States and shares a home with seven feral cats. This is one of them:

CURSING SILENTLY, **K**AT scratched frantically for a finger-hold on the slick ceramic skin of the ship. But the surface was flawlessly smooth, without even so much as a seam or rivet point.

She was sliding faster now; she had no tools left to slow her velocity in the frictionless void of space. The hull passed by so quickly beneath her desperate grasp it was a blur.

To make matters worse, the farther she slid the more steeply the hull declined as the stern gently curved downwards. In a minute she wouldn't just be skidding over the smooth surface, she would actually leave it and drift off into space. She would already have floated off if it weren't for the ship's weak gravity that still gently pulled her.

But even now she could feel her every frantic scratch pushing her off just a little bit more.

The stern of the ship rushed toward her at breakneck speed. It was now a matter of mere seconds.

When the moment did come she almost couldn't tell. She was no longer in contact with the hull, and one second she was watching it zip by her plummeting form, and the next she had passed it and dropped off helplessly into the void.

She tilted her head back and saw the underbelly of the huge starship above her. As she slowly started to rotate end over end, she watched the ship move lower in her vision while her body did a slow-motion backflip in the darkness. Just as the last image of the ship disappeared behind her feet she heard the chime in her helmet as her suit announced, "All oxygen has been expended. System shutting down."

And her helmet – along with the rest of her suit – went dark.

THEY LEAVE ME for dead, lying in a drainage ditch beside the road, and I can hear them as they drive away in my car, just a couple of good ol' boys lighting cigarettes and cracking jokes, as though they're coming back from a fishing trip and not from having just beaten someone to death.

I can't tell you how long I lie here, listening to the rain and the wind and the crickets and all the assorted night sounds that creep back to life after the humans have gone. The stentorian gasps of my own ragged breathing keep time with the persistent rustle of some weeds just off to my left, making me wonder if perhaps some hungry wild creature is assessing my potential as a snack. I am slipping into and out of consciousness every few minutes, and in a grey recess of my mind I peripherally hope that I will be insensate when the beast finally decides to start gnawing on whichever part of my body it's going to eat first.

Every so often a vehicle shoots by in the night, announcing itself first with the quiet hiss of its approach, then gradually crescendoing into a deafening rattling roar defining its identity as car, pickup truck, or 18-wheeler. The weeds around my head sway and buck convulsively as the vehicle whizzes past my location, and then in the wake of its passage quickly resume their motionless witness to my suffering.

I have no way to alert the passing drivers to my presence. I can't seem to move my arms and legs, or even turn my head, either because some part of my spine is damaged or merely just because the intense pain from the rest of my body is overwhelming all my other senses.
I know that several of my ribs are broken, along with at least two of the fingers on my left hand. My sides throb in excruciating pain, and I assume that I am bleeding internally from several damaged organs. I can't really see at all from either of my eyes, as both are swollen shut and caked in blood. The taste of blood fills my mouth and I can't breathe through my nose.

I lie here, face down in the dirt and muck, and I wait – for death, or the dawn. I have no way of knowing which will arrive first.

Literati International
~ Since 1984 ~
Toronto • New York • London

Literati International is the privately-held parent company of Literati Media, established in 1984 in Toronto, Canada, which comprises Literati Worldwide Publications, Literati Broadcasting Enterprises, Literati International Reporting & Podcast Productions, and Literati Film and Television Post-Production Services.

Literati International has affiliate partnerships and representatives in numerous countries around the globe, including Australia, India, and Brazil.

Check out the full line of Literati-produced books and media at www.literatiinternational.com

www.ingramcontent.com/pod-product-compliance
Lightning Source LLC
Chambersburg PA
CBHW070643100726
47907CB00007B/2092